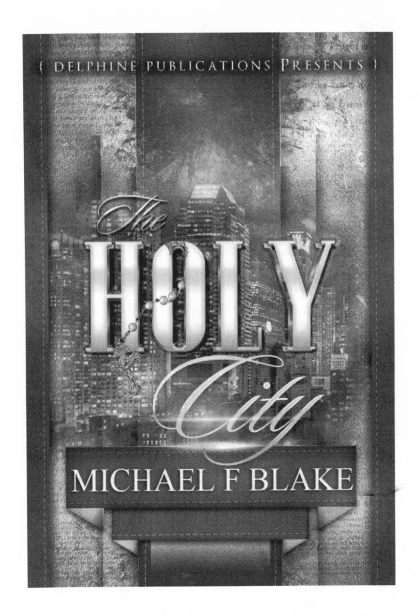

{ DELPHINE PUBLICATIONS Presents }

The HOLY City

MICHAEL F BLAKE

The Holy City

Delphine Publications focuses on bringing a reality check to the genre urban literature.
All stories are a work of fiction from the authors and are not meant to depict, portray, or represent any particular person.

Names, characters, places, and incidents are either the product of the author's imagination or are used fictitiously, and any resemblances to an actual person living or dead are entirely coincidental.

The Holy City
© 2013 Michael F. Blake

ISBN 13 - 978-0988709317

Cover Design: Odd Ball Designs
Layout: Write On Promotions

Published by Delphine Publications
www.DelphinePublications.com

Printed in the United States of America

Dedication

This book is dedicated to the loving memory of Emma Brown, my grandmother. When she left, so did a piece of my heart. I love you, Bay!

Acknowledgements

First and foremost I would like to praise GOD for watching over me and showing me the way. I never thought I would become a writer and to be honest, at times I was ready to give up. But I stayed prayed up an every time; the LORD gave me the strength to keep going forward. GOD always sent signs my way to assure me that I was definitely in the "blessing line". Thank You GOD for exposing such a great hidden talent within me: I'm nothing without YOU!

I want to thank my mother, Kelly Blake, for loving me and installing entrepreneurship inside of me at an early age. She always drilled in my head to create work for myself. She never allowed me to believe that there was a future in working a job. To this day having a nine-to-five job has never been in my repertoire!

I would like to thank my pops, Michael "Pee Wee" Brown for being there for me as a child and for being understanding and supportive on most decisions that I made throughout my life, good or bad. My father set an example early on in my life on how to always conduct myself with class in anything that I do. I can always count on his advice when it came to the women and the streets.

I would like to give special thanks to Bonnie Blake, my grandmother, for helping raise me to become the man that I am today; I love you for that!

Last but surely not least, I would like to give a heartfelt thank-you to the two loves of my life, Michael "Mikey" Blake Jr. and his beautiful mother (my future wife) Marqueta Williams, for their love and support throughout my entire bid behind these walls. Second to god, they gave me the strength I needed to thrive on upon completing this project; I appreciate y'all from the bottom of my heart.

With much Honor and Respect

I want to give special thanks to the past and present community leaders of the "Holy City". Without y'all this story would not have been possible to recite.

To my uncle, you know who you is, for sacrificing most of your life to the struggle, making it possible for me to have something worth remembering and talking about; I luv you for that. Unc, I hope I make you proud with this one.

To my oldest cousin Tim for exposing the harsh reality of the street life, live and direct! Coming up in the same household and being around you all my life allowed me to pick up on some valuable lessons in the game that helped me become the stand up guy that I am today.

To my cousin Donald a.k.a Don-Don for never keeping secrets and always keeping it real with me, Keep doing you cuz, luv you boy!

To my cousin Zayboo for being with me throughout our entire upbringing; All the shit we've seemed coming up, I'm sure you got plenty of movies in your head to write about ya' dam self! Even though we grew apart and had our differences, you still my brother for life.

To my cousin Akili a.k.a Ke-Ke for being the brother I never had; for always understanding the bullshit that was going on in my life when nobody else did. I know you're out there in that wicked world and can't focus like you need to but you got to fight through it and get your mind right.

To my lil sister Kelisha a.k.a Keli B for being the first person in our immediate family to showcase raw talent, Thanks for allowing me to help jump start your musical career. Our journey is yet to be over. Sometimes we fall down only to get back up stronger and better.

To Big Mike you made my life fun, thanks for always being around, good looking out.

Everyone I just named personally influenced me in some shape, form or fashion. I will never forget all the fine memories we gave one another over the years. Much, much luv!

Shout outs'

I want to give shout outs' to my entire Blake Family. Uncle Truel Sr. Rest in Peace, your name will forever live on. Aunt-tee Re-Re, Selena and Charlene luv you ladies. Uncle August a.k.a Road Dawg, keep ya' head up I hope and pray that you see the street soon, I understand ya' pain; Uncle Steve, Chris and Ralph keep doing you. Chris Jr. and Janelle luv ya'. Deon, I appreciate you cuz for having my back and helping me out through some pretty tough times, you was there when a nigga hit rock bottom in them streets. Mrs. Betty McKnight a.k.a Grandma, no matter what, I will never forget you taking the time to come visit me when you didn't have to, I love you much! All my little cousin I didn't mention, I love y'all too! To the entire Spivey Family, there's no way I could name everyone but please know that you all have a place in my heart.

I want to give a holla to my entire Brown Family, Uncle Junior! Uncle Doll, I will never forget the trips to the Dells and the wrestling matches you took us to when we were younger, I appreciate you reaching out to me during my darkest times. Mr. Dee, Whudd up Kidd! I can always count on you to be ya'self at all time. To all the Brown family I didn't mention, I love y'all too . . . To my two brothers Detron and Miguel stay focus.

To all my comrades that held me down in my day to day struggle in the joint, Big Gee, I see you boy, Kwame Boyd, Lord Dre from the wild hunits, wassup hometown! My nigga Cee P, we'll definitely hook up, War-town, keep spitting that hot shit, Shamel Jackson a.k.a Gipp, I see you blood, my lil nigga Rico a.k.a Mac-town, being the first person to read the rough draft and push me hard to complete this project and that meant a lot to me. Devon, straight out of Macon GA a.k.a Mac, Randy Leonard, Nubs a.k.a Mo, Big Lew.

The

Holy

City

PROLOGUE

"Marcus . . . Marcus! You don't hear Momma back there calling you," said Chris, his younger brother, as they both sat on the steps of their front porch enjoying a nice summer morning in June.

"Huuuhhh!" Marcus responded to his mother's calling as he snapped out of a trance

"Boy, you didn't hear me back here calling you?" Sylvia yelled as she stood at the back door in her famous all-black satin nightgown. "Get in here and take out this garbage. You know it's too damn hot to be letting this trash pile up like that!"

"A'ight, here I come!" Marcus replied, still not making a move toward the door. "Mannnnn, that nigga gettin' money," Marcus said in a hushed tone while staring at Smitty glide down their street in his drop-top cocaine-white '79 El Dorado Cadillac with maroon leather interior, bangin' Al Green's "Love and Happiness" on his sound system that was so loud that you could actually hear him coming from three blocks away.

Honk! Honk! Was the sound of Smitty horn as he acknowledged the two brothers by throwing up the deuce.

"Yeah, that nigga know who I am," Marcus muttered out with confidence as he threw up the deuce while staring at Smitty slowly drive down their block.

"What make you think he knows you, you ain't nobody," Chris sarcastically blurted out.

"What! You saw how that nigga looked over here. He know wassup wit' me."

"The only reason he looked this way because he know Daddy stay here," Chris said as he began to ease off the porch onto the sidewalk.

"Remember, that's yo' punk-ass daddy, not min," Marcus replied offensively.

"Ahhhh! You mad 'cause don't nobody know you, dude!" Chris taunted in a teasingly fashion while heading in the direction of one of his friends' house two doors down.

"A'ight, we gon' see 'who know who' when I start gettin' this money."

"Don't worry, that ain't gon' happen no time soon," said Chris as he continued to pick at his older brother.

"Marcus!" Sylvia yelled harshly from out the house.

"Okay, here I come!" Marcus quickly responded with a slight attitude as he reached out for the door while looking back at Chris.

On his dreadful walk into the house, Marcus was mumbling some pretty unpleasant words under his breath until his mother interrupted his train of thought.

"How many times do I have to call your name for you to get in here and do what the hell I told you to do?!" Sylvia snapped as she stood in the kitchen with her hands resting on her hips.

Even though Sylvia only stood about four foot ten, she demanded her respect from anyone that associated themselves with her, especially men. Sylvia was determined not to allow her kids to disrespect her, but at times, she would show a little leniency toward their smart remarks.

"You should've asked that nigga to do it," Marcus mumbled under his breath while grabbing the bag out the trash can.

"What'chú say?" Sylvia asked vigorously after seeing movement come from his lips.

"Nuttin'."

"I told you 'bout that smart-ass mouth of yours. You gon' make me slap the taste out it! Keep on getting smart!" Sylvia threatened while mean mugging Marcus as he was leaving out the back door with the trash.

"Man, I can't stand her ass. Soon's I get me some bread I'm gettin' the fuck out her house!" Marcus said in an aggressive whisper while carrying the trash bag over his shoulder on the way to the alley.

As Marcus continued to walk and talk to himself, he didn't notice someone creep up behind him.

"Give that shit up, homey . . . ," was a disguised voice coming directly from behind Marcus. "You didn't hear what the fuck I said, give that shit up!"

"Damn, man, I ain't got shit but some trash, homey," Marcus nervously pleaded.

"Ahhhh! You was shook like a muthafucka!" Pee Wee said while tucking his pistol back into his waistline. Pee Wee was one of Marcus's main buddies.

"What the fuck you around here playing like that for! That playing shit gon' get'cho ass fucked up!" Marcus said while looking Pee Wee square in the eyes.

"Damn, homey, I was jus' messin' wit'chú, you a'ight?" Pee Wee asked with a smirk.

"I'm straight," Marcus said while attempting to calm his nerves. "My momma jus' blowin' the shit out me early this morning."

Marcus began to stroll back toward the house with a slight frown on his face from the thought of facing his mother again once making it in the house.

"What time you coming back out?" Pee Wee asked as he strolled behind.

"In'a minute," he responded without looking back.

"Yea right. You know damn well Steve ain't gon' let'cho ass back outside," Pee Wee jokingly commented, knowing that his statement would aggravate Marcus.

Marcus simply shook his head at what was said as he dreaded going back in the house. Once making it inside, Marcus instantly went to his room that he shared with Chris. He then grabbed his underclothes and headed toward the bathroom to take a shower, only to see that it was being occupied by Steve taking a shower.

"Shit!" Marcus sighed angrily. Any small thing that Steve did irritated the hell out of Marcus. "Ma!" Marcus yelled out for his mother in a sympathetic tone of voice as he began marching toward her room.

"What?"

"Can you gimme a couple dolla's, please?" he asked, trying to sound sincere as possible.

"For what?" Sylvia countered irritably.

"When I get dressed, me, Marlin, and JR goin' up to the arcade room on Sixteenth." Marcus knew which ones of his friends' names to mention. If he would've said anything about Pee Wee or Lil G, she might've rejected the whole idea, quick! Sylvia attended high school with JR's and Marlin's mothers, so they kept tabs on each other's kid. Lil G and Pee Wee had only been around the neighborhood for a couple of years, and they already had long rap sheets. Sylvia knew about their troubles, so she never knowingly allowed Marcus to hang out with them.

"I don't have it. You know the first of the month jus' passed and I had to catch up on my bills. Knock on the bathroom door and ask Steve for a few dollars. I'm sure he'll give it to you." She said all of this while looking in the mirror, combing her long wavy sandy brown hair.

Marcus left the room sucking air between his teeth from his mother's request. Out of all people, Steve was the last person on earth that he wanted to ask for something from; even though there was a possibility that Steve would give it to him. There was something about Steve that Marcus wasn't feeling.

What the hell. All he can say is no, Marcus thought to himself.

"Hey, Steve, you think I could—"

"I ain't got no money," Steve cut him off from making his statement as he walked toward their mother's room with just a little towel wrapped around his waist.

Marcus walked back to his room, cursing Steve out under his breath, "I knew I shouldn't have asked that nigga for shit. I don't even fuck wit' him like dat." Marcus muttered out in a low-pitched tone of voice.

Marcus didn't let his mother or Steve spoil his plans to go outside. After jumping out the shower and making it to his room, he impatiently brushed through his dresser drawers, looking for something fresh to wear outside. Everything he pulled out, he threw back into the drawer because either he had worn a certain outfit too many times or it simply wasn't intriguing enough to him.

"Damn, man, I ain't got shit to put on!" Marcus said aggressively while picking out his cleanest pair of shorts and shirt that matched. "I don't even wanna wear this shit!" he continued to complain to himself, obviously feeling frustrated from how his day had already begun.

Once Marcus put on his clothes, he proceeded to go outside. He managed to get over being denied money because it wasn't the first time he had been turned down when he asked for something. You could tell from Marcus's reactions lately that he was growing tired of being rejected.

When Marcus stepped foot out the front door, he looked around to see that the block was filled with everyone who lived on Hamlin. Marcus began strolling down the street going toward Cermak Road, heading in the direction of the Twenty-first Strip, which was five blocks down from Cermak and Hamlin. Before he could make it to Cermak, Marcus saw his little brother sitting on one of his friends' porch, eating some snacks from the store.

"Where you get some money from?" Marcus asked while rudely snatching a bag of chips out of Chris's hands.

"From my daddy, why?" Chris asked with a frown.

"When he give it to you?"

"Just a few minutes ago befo' he jumped in the car wit' Big C."

"How much he hit'chú wit'?" Marcus asked curiously.

"Twenty dolla's," Chris replied mockingly

"Let me borrow a fin?"

"A'ight . . . ," Chris said as he reached into his pocket. "You better pay me back my five dolla's, too!" Chris demanded as if he was the older of the two.

"I got'chú," Marcus responded as he was accepting the money from his younger brother. Of course Marcus had no intentions of paying Chris back anytime soon.

Just when Marcus cooled down, his frustration arose again once he had to borrow money from his little brother.

"Ain't this some shit, here I am the big brother gettin' money from my little brother. Man this some straight bullsh—"

"Aey, Marcus!" a loud voice from afar yelled, breaking Marcus from his train of thoughts.

Marcus squinched his eyes to see who was calling him. "Awe, that's Lil

G . . . ," Marcus said to himself. "Wudd up!" he hollered down the street with his arms raised in the air. As they continued to walk, they met up with each other halfway down Cermak on the corner of Lawndale. "Wassup, Jo," Marcus greeted Lil G by performing the IVL handshake.

"Shhit . . . Tired than a muthafucka. Been on the block hustlin' all night," Said Lil G as he stretched and yawned. Lil G was a couple of years older than Marcus, and he was full-fledged in the streets.

"Where you was on yo' way to?" Lil G asked.

"I was fenna' walk over on Twenty-first to fuck wit' y'all."

"Everybody up at the arcade room. You know that's where all the hoes at right now," Lil G said, shaking his head up and down with a smile.

"A'ight then . . . I'll jus' catch up wit' y'all later on," Marcus said in an upsetting tone as he began walking off.

"What'chú mean?" Lil G asked while looking puzzled. "You ain't coming up there?"

"I'm fucked up, Jo. I ain't got no bread."

"Maaannn . . . come 'ere, lord!" Lil G called Marcus back as he continued to walk.

"Wassup." Marcus turned around and slowly walked back.

"You know as long as I got it, you straight," Lil G claimed as

he entered both of his front pockets, pulling out a thick stack of cash from each pocket. Lil G looked through both stacks of money while whispering to himself as if he was sorting out which stack was for what.

"Okay," Lil G mumbled to himself as he put one stack back in his pocket. "Here you go my nigga." He peeled off six twenty-dollar bills to give Marcus.

"Nah, I can't 'cept yo' hard earned money, Jo." He reacted by shaking his head.

"Listen, man . . . If you ain't gon' accept my money and we homies, then you need to get out here and get it yo' self. Even though we young, I still hate to see a real nigga like you out here strugglin' when I kno' you got this street shit in you. Shhiiit, you prob'le stronger than all us put together." Lil G laughed, forcing a smirk upon Marcus's face as he stuffed the money into his hand.

Marcus stood there in a daze for a minute as he thought about the promise he made to himself after his father was murdered. He promised himself that he would never get caught up in the street life. He was now contemplating on whether or not the early choice he made in life was the best fit for his well-being.

"Marcus, Marcus," Lil G repeated, attempting to get Marcus out of a deep thought. "Ya a'ight?"

"Yeah, yeah, I'm straight," he said with a confused expression upon his face as he stuffed the money into his pocket.

"Come-on, Jo, let's go get us some weed and get up on these hoes down here at the arcade."

"Yeah I'm wit it, let's ride," Marcus said while still looking confused.

Chapter 1

It was the fall of '89, the year when the Chicago Bulls weren't able to get past their archrivals, the Detroit Pistons. Christopher was a die-hard Bulls fan, so these weren't the glory days for his team. On the other hand, Marcus cared less about sports; it didn't matter to him who was winning in the world of sports at that time. They were living in a household of four: Sylvia Williams, the mother of the two; Christopher at the age of ten and Marcus at the age of sixteen were the two brothers; Steven Brown, the longtime boyfriend of Sylvia and also the father of Chris.

From day one there had been conflict in the household between Marcus and Steve. Marcus never liked the fact that his mother was in love with a street dude. Steve had done two separate bids in the penitentiary within the years that he was involved with Sylvia, and she accepted him back each time with open arms. Marcus always thought his mother could do better in her choice of men, especially after his father was victimized due to street activities. With that said, you can say Marcus always held a grudge against Steve on the low. By all means Chris loved his daddy to death; I mean Steve couldn't do anything wrong in his young eyes. Chris was very naive at an early age.

Sylvia, although she was a small woman, worked two jobs to make ends meet. Even though Steve was in the streets hustling, she never depended on him to take care of her. Of course he would give her money for whatever was needed. Steve wasn't making major money at the time, but he was making enough to maintain.

One day while getting dressed for school, both brothers had different attires. Marcus didn't have the type of gear that was required amongst his peers, which was a fresh Girbaud outfit and whatever new pair of Jordan's that was out at the time. On the other hand, Chris stayed fresh in a pair of Jordan's or some Nike Air Flights; he was only in the fifth grade. Sylvia never really believed in fashion, so all the fresh gear Chris was getting came from his father. A form of jealousy was starting to settle inside Marcus. He even started skipping school just because his gear wasn't up to par. These years was the era where gangbangin' was very tough in the neighborhood. If you were in the streets, either you were a part of a nation or you were a nobody!

Christopher stood five foot three and played basketball for the school he attended (St. Angela, a Catholic school that's located on the Near West Side of Chicago). Chris was a stocky kid that sported a box cut with a high-top fade for his hairstyle. He was an average student that had all the attention from the young ladies because of his handsome, innocent young face and his million-dollar smile that would almost ignite anyone. Marcus stood about five foot nine and was also husky built and had the physical strength of an adult. Despite Marcus having a street mentality, he definitely was a ladies' man.

Young women loved his caramel skin tone and his low cut that was covered with silky waves. Marcus had hair on his face at an early age; he even grew out a full beard. Sometimes he would attract older women with his appearance. Marcus also attended the Catholic school before getting expelled in the fifth grade for fighting. Sylvia then transferred him to a public school not too far from their house, where fighting was a regular. Somehow he made it through and graduated from the eighth grade.

Steve was an athletic man who stood about five foot eleven with a dark brown complexion. Back in the day, he was the star basketball player for his high school. He also went on to play two years of college ball at Ohio State. All his hoop dreams came to an end one summer while he was home from college. He was playing in a basketball tournament in the 'hood, came down wrong on someone's foot, and broke his ankle. After that incident, his

2

basketball career was never the same. Steve had always been an affiliate with the Conservative Vice Lord Nation, but soon after his hoop dreams were deflated by injuries, he began putting in a lot of work in the streets for guys that was higher ranked in the nation. Steve was no doubt a coldhearted gangster, but with the swagger of a ballplayer. People in the 'hood labeled him as a street ball legend because of all the goals he had accomplished on the court. He would destroy any NBA player that would come back home to Chicago for the summer to play in the 'hood tournaments.

Marcus's dad was killed in a bad drug deal when Marcus was only five years old. His dad was also a street dude whose main focus wasn't selling drugs; his forte was more on robbing big-time drug dealers in the 'hood. Marcus's father and Steve knew of each other when they were coming up in the streets but never came in contact with one another. When Sylvia and Big Marc (Marcus's father) split up, not long after, she and Steve met; then eventually they started dating. When Big Marc learned about Sylvia getting serious with another man, let alone someone from around the way, it didn't sit too well with him at all. In fact, it was rumored in the streets that Big Marc's last robbery victim was affiliated with Steve and his organization. Big Marc hit for a nice amount of money and work. It was said that he took thirty thousand and two kilos of raw cocaine from one of their stash houses. Supposedly, Steve knew about the bad drug deal that was set up to have Big Marc killed. The meeting was set up through a mutual associate of theirs, who was later found dead soon after Big Marc's murder. Marcus at the age of five was too young at the time to know about street news, but the streets do talk, and as Marcus got older, his ear began to hit the streets. Years later he learned about the street rumor through an ole head that ran with his pops back in the day. Marcus informed his mother about the story, and she rejected it and told Marcus to keep quiet. From that point on, Marcus began having mixed feelings about Steve.

Marcus was a freshman at Farragut High School. This would be the only year that he would attend school. He caught his first charge at school during a fight between two girls. It was said that Marcus pulled the shirt off one girl. He got arrested, and eventually he was expelled. Marcus got expelled from two other high schools after that. It was to the point that no other schools in the Chicago land area would accept him.

Soon later, Marcus was blessed into the IVLN (Insane Vice Lord Nation). Their set was based along the Twenty-first Strip. Twenty-first was five blocks from where he lived. The strip consisted of five main blocks: St. Louis, Trumbull, Homan, Christiana, and Spaulding. Twenty-first was ran under one nation in the late '80s and early '90s and had only one chief, whose name was Smitty. Smitty was the commander in chief of anyone in the city of Chicago who claimed to be under the IVL nation. Smitty was medium built with a brown complexion and always kept a cold expression on his face. His eyes were dark and cold, like someone who had seen many horror scenes in his lifetime. He stood about five foot ten and sported a ball head. Smitty always moved in silence, but when he came for you, you felt his presence tremendously!

Right under Smitty was the five-star universal, whose name was Spoonie. Spoonie was short, black as hell, and looked harmless. Although Spoonie looked harmless enough, he was anything but that. He was one of Smitty most effective enforcer at that time. Each area Smitty had control over had its own leaders, in which they were called three-star elites. Block leaders were the ones under them who made sure all the money was on point after every shift. Each block had shifts: morning shift (5:00 a.m. till 11:00 a.m.), day shift (12:00 p.m. to 8:00 p.m.), and overnight shift (9:00 p.m. to 4:00 a.m.).

The main supply of drugs in the area was heroin a.k.a. blows or dope. The other drug was fairly new in the 'hood in the '80s, redi-rock a.k.a. crack. Each one of the four blocks on the Twenty-first Strip made roughly twenty thousand a night. This was just one area out of several that Smitty had control over.

Smitty was the type of chief that made all of his soldiers follows strict rules. If some of the younger lords were still going to school, they wouldn't be able to hustle until school hours were over. If any man thought they were bigger than the nation, a violation usually took place. Some violations were more severe than others; it depended on the case. The number one rule of all rules was to never, I mean never, under any circumstances, snitch on any man, not even your worst enemy! If Smitty had any doubt in his mind that someone in the nation was cooperating with the police, he would order an MOS hit (murder on sight!).

Marcus was well aware of how the organization worked because all of his friends had joined. His friends were basically under the same circumstances, if not, theirs were worse; mother on drugs and/or either they didn't know their father, or he was dead or in jail. Marcus had five main friends that he ran with daily: Marlin, Pee Wee, JR, Lil G, and Mikey. Marcus had a different mentality than all of them; his mentality was more of a leader than a follower. All of his buddies never minded being followers. In the past, Marcus always called a few of his friends stupid for selling dope packs on the block, until one day Marcus was ordered to be brought to the attention of Spoonie.

Chapter 2

"Wudd up, lord?" Marcus greeted Marlin by performing the nation's handshake as he walked up on Twenty-first and Homan. The sun was setting, going into nightfall, and the block was accumulating major traffic—from cars speeding through the block, some cars stopping in the middle of the street holding up traffic talking to people they knew, even hypes flooding the block for drugs.

"Wudd up wit'chú, homey," Marlin responded, with his undivided attention being on all the activities that was going on in front of him. In the same breath, he hollered out, "Aey! Y'all hurry up and move all that traffic, man. People tryn'a get through! These stupid-ass niggaz gon' get a nigga popped off out here with this dumb shit." He said this as he and Marcus gradually walked down Homan.

"Aey, aey, who workin'?" asked a neighborhood dope fiend who frantically walked up while impatiently flashing his money.

"What'chú need?" Marlin quickly reacted.

"Five rocks, five blows," the fiend anxiously stated.

"Go to the middle of the block. I'll be down 'nere in a minute," Marlin explained while in the midst of making a move toward his stash. "Aey, lord, stay right there. I'll be right back," he hollered out to Marcus as he jogged off.

While Marlin was taking care of business, Marcus stood there and witnessed him dictate traffic and receive more money from the growing customers that kept walking up. No matter how much Marcus wanted to hide his desire to hustle, he couldn't deny the passion that filled him as he watched Marlin and the others on the block handle business.

"A'ight, let's ride," Marlin announced once making it back in the presence of Marcus.

"Gaddamn, I was about to walk off and leave yo' ass. Got me standin' out here like a sitting duck on this hot-ass block," Marcus said with a sense of humor.

"Ain't nobody got'chú out here. I don't understand how you be out here all the time and not be tryn'a get some of this paper!" Marlin said with excitement as they strolled down Homan going in the direction of the main street, Twenty-first.

"Man, I ain't tryn'a be out here workin' packs!"

"You ain't gotta be workin' packs . . . I mean, you gotta start from somewhere. I don't work packs all the time, but I be needin' that quick money. Shhhiiit, you see how much traffic be coming through Homan . . . ," Marlin said while counting all the money he made from the day shift.

"Aey, walk down here with me so I can meet up wit' Spoonie, I gotta holla' at him about some'nt."

"A'ight, let's go," Marcus responded without any hesitation.

On their walk down Twenty-first, Marlin emptied out a White Owl blunt and filled it with weed. Almost every car that drove past them blew their horn and threw up the deuce. The Twenty-first Strip was one of the many places where the vice lords roamed, so everybody that was affiliated knew each other.

As they continued to walk and smoke, they periodically stopped to fool around with certain females and guys from the neighborhood.

"Aey Jessica! Bring yo' ball head ass ova' here!" Marlin jokingly yelled across the street at a group of young females walking down Twenty-first whom he normally talked shit to on a daily basis.

"Boa, I know yo' lil dirty ass ain't over there talkin' 'bout me wit' them same clothes you had on from two days ago!"

Everyone in her group busted out in laughter as she yelled back, matching Marlin's humor.

"I'll be dirty as long as I keep that dirty money in my pocket!" he responded by cockily holding up a stack of cash.

"That ain't shit!" Jessica continued. "It prob'le ain't nuttin' but a twenty on top of a bunch of one's, wit'cho' broke ass!"

"Yeah right, I—"

"Aey, look at Donisha lil sexy ass," Marcus said in a hushed tone, as he continuously tapped Marlin on the arm, interrupting him from making a smart remark.

"Maaann, fuck dat bitch. She think she all that since she been fuckin' one of Spoonie guys. You know dat nigga Reggie, don't you?"

"Man, fuck all that. Aye, Donisha! Slow up!" Marcus hollered out, getting the group's attention as they continued to march down Twenty-first.

"What!" Donisha hollered back from a distance with a slight attitude.

"Come 'ere for a minute!"

As she reluctantly turned around and headed back down the street, she blurted out, "Meet me halfway. I ain't walkin' all the way back down there!" Donisha was the most attractive girl out of the group. Although she was only sixteen, she had the body of a woman in her twenties. She kept her hair done in a dark brown weave wrap that offset her smooth pecan-colored skin tone. Unlike the other girls in their crew, she was blessed at an early age with nice thick shapely thighs with a slight gap in between her legs that matched her wide-spreaded hips, along with a perfect backside that complimented all her attributes. To top everything off, she kept her full juicy lips glossed up to perfection.

"Damn, girl, you jus' gon' make me chase after you, huh?" Marcus said while being slightly out of breath from jogging a half block. "Wasssup wit'chú, Don?"

"Shit, 'bout to walk ova' on Christiana so they can get them some weed," she said nonchalantly. "You know I'mma good girl. I don't be smokin' that shit like y'all. Look at' cho' ass, high as hell right now!" she said while giggling and shaking her head at Marcus's attempt to straighten his facial expression

"Girl, you know you stay lookin' good."

"You know a bitch gotta stay fly," she said in a sassy fashion with her hands resting on her hips while glancing down at her gear, which consisted of a pink and white halter top that barely covered her stomach, with a seductive phrase written on the front, and some blue jean shorts that was so tight, they weren't able to pass her upper thighs. She sported some new all-white Reebok classics with the footie's that had the pink fuzzy ball on the back.

As they continued to make small talk with each other, Marcus stood there, slowly eyeing her down from head to toe. From the expression Marcus had on his face, it was obvious that he was high, and all he could think of was how badly he wanted to sex Donisha down!

"When you gon' let me—"

"Let chú what!" she cut him off while raising one eyebrow at his half statement.

"I mean, you know, when you gon' have some time to kick it wit' me," Marcus replied with hesitation as if he was correcting himself.

"You see me damn near every day. All you gotta do is come walk wit' us."

"Nah, I'm talkin' 'bout us kickin' it alone, you know, so we can talk and get to know each other a lil betta'."

"Nigga, you been knowin' me the whole two years I been stayin' around here wit' my auntie."

"You kno' what I'm sayin'."

"Yeah, I kno' whatchú' tryn'a say. That's why you need to say whatchú feel and quit beatin' 'round the bush."

"Bitch! You need to hurry up 'fore we leave yo' ass!" One of Donisha's rowdy friends yelled from a block away.

"Look, Marcus, you cool and everything but I'm seein' somebody right now," she said while backing her way down the street.

Marcus stood there for a minute in a daze while watching Donisha swing her hips, with her ass seductively moving from side to side as she walked down the street, knowing that she had his attention.

"Damn, she don't know what I'a do to her," Marcus mumbled to himself with a sexual desire as he began to walk off.

Marlin was leaning against a parked car, smoking on a Newport, conversing with one of the brothers from off Sixteenth Street that previously drove up.

"Dee Jay, drop us off on Cermak and Springfield," Marlin demanded. Before Deejay could give an answer, Marlin and Marcus were already jumping into his Chevy Caprice.

"Gurrrl, what the hell Marcus want wit'chu?" Jessica asked in a snappy tone of voice.

"Yo' guess is as good as mine. I think he was tryn'a holla'. I mean, he cute and everything, but if a nigga ain't gettin' to that paper, he ain't got'a chance in hell wit' me!"

"Bitch! You talkin' like you all dat!" one of the girls aggressively blurted out, making everyone in the group laugh as they kept on about their business.

Dee Jay was a pack runner for the conservatives off Sixteenth. He was the type of nigga that damn near knew everybody in the 'hood because of how cool he was.

After making a detour to stop and buy some weed, Dee Jay drove through a few extra blocks while they smoked. The Chevy he was driving in was the block car.

"Damn, Jo, dis raggedy ma'fucka be ridin' don't it," Marlin teased as he took a long drag off the blunt while listening to the latest mixtape.

"Hell yeah, nigga, I'll put this ma'fucka up against any Chevy in the 'hood!"

"Nigga, you crazy as hell, dis ma'fucka a' cut off befo' you even make it through the race!" They all laughed from the comment.

"Anyway, Marcus, I saw u hollin' at dat lil freak everybody been tryn'a get at. Wassup wit' her?" Deejay asked as he glanced to the backseat at Marcus.

"I mean, she cool, but'chú know how these hoes be frontin'," Marcus said while reaching for the blunt that was being passed to him from the front seat.

"Man, Jo, I told you that hoe wasn't on shit," Marlin stated while coughing from the weed smoke. "She jus' looks for a nigga to take care her ass. I can tell jus' by lookin' at her."

Marcus didn't say a word as they continued to smoke and ride.

"Man, you jus' passed Springfield three times," Marlin said.

"The blunt ain't gon' yet."

"Man, fuck dat. I told you I had to take care some business. Let us out right here, we a walk to the block."

They got out of the car and walked a block down to Springfield while finishing the blunt.

"I 'posed to been met this nigga down here thirty minutes ago. I hope he still ova' here," Marlin said as they turned the corner.

As soon as they turned the block, they witnessed a crowd of people standing outside, laughing and talking to one another. As they got a little closer, they recognized it was Spoonie entertaining the crowd, with Lil G and Pee Wee standing beside him.

"Damn, nigga, it took you long enuff," Spoonie said jokingly while turning his attention toward the two. "You must think I ain't got moves to make or some'nt."

Earlier that day, Spoonie ordered Marlin to bring Marcus around him later on, but he didn't want Marcus to know what the matter was. Spoonie wanted to talk to him about a business proposition. He knew Marcus had the ability and traits in his blood to be more than just a gangbanger; he had it in him to be a great earner for the nation, and after putting in enough work, he could become a made nigga. Spoonie knew Marcus was smarter than the average young dude.

"Lil G, where y'all been at all day?" Marlin asked.

"Ova' here fuckin' around," Lil G responded with a feel-good expression on his face with a small clear plastic cup in his hand with a green potion inside. It was obvious that it was vodka and lime juice from the loud scent.

"Let me get a sip," Marlin demanded while reaching and taking the cup from him. Marcus followed suit by doing the same thing to Pee Wee.

This was the type of relationship the six of them established, including JR and Mikey when they were around. When any one of them had anything in their possession—as far as liquor, weed, or girls that they didn't care too much about—they shared with each other with no problem.

In the meanwhile, while the four of them was laughing and joking amongst each other, Spoonie was off to the side conversing on the phone. Spoonie had a couple of other guys nearby, when an Astro van pulled up banging some house music (a certain type of dance music that was made popular in Chicago in the '80s and early '90s). Spoonie stood there on the phone; with no surprise, his buddy Reggie jumped out the van. Spoonie had been expecting him to pull up for a minute so they could talk and take care of some business.

"My fault, lord!" Reggie exclaimed as he got out the van and started walking toward Spoonie. "My bitch had me held up at the crib arguing over some stupid shit."

"It's all good. Next time tell yo' lady if she wonna keep eating good, it'll be smart for her to let'chú out on time." They both laughed and shook up with each other.

Reggie was what you called a pretty-boy thug. He stood about five foot ten; medium built, light skinned, and sported a curly 'fro with a low fade on the sides. Reggie was more of a hustler than a gangster, even though he was affiliated with the TVL nation (Traveler Vice Lord, another street organization). Despite his good looks, how well he dressed, and what people thought of him, if his back was against the wall, he'll bust his gun with no questions asked.

"Aey, go down in tha' basement. I got Tameka down 'nere waitin' on you so y'all can count dat money you got for me. When y'all get through countin', she gon' give you whatchú need, a'ight," Spoonie instructed.

"Damn, I gotta count all this bread wit' her," Reggie said as he turned to walk toward the van to get the money. "You gon' make me miss out on this bad lil' broad I got waitin' on me, lord!" he said jokingly, knowing Spoonie cared less about a female when it came down to taking care of business.

Tameka was a heavyset tomboy that Spoonie had on his team. She had strength like a man and was more loyal than some niggaz in the streets. Spoonie used her basement apartment sometimes to take care of business.

"Aey, Marcus, come 'ere!" Spoonie hollered over to where the crowd stood.

"Wassup," Marcus said as he walked up.

"Shit, wassup wit'chú, lord?" Spoonie asked as if he was trying to ease Marcus's nerves as they shook up.

"Chillin', out here trippin' wit' these fools."

"Lord, I'mma cut right to the chase . . . What'chú gon' do, Jo?" Spoonie asked while sparking up a blunt that he had resting on his ear.

"What'chú mean?" Marcus asked curiously.

"What I mean is . . . we blessed you in, right?"

"Right," Marcus answered

"Why you ain't out there tryn'a hustle. What, you gettin' money from somewhere else and ain't tellin' us? If you is, I sho'll can't tell." Spoonie grinned as he took another pull off the blunt while looking Marcus up and down.

"Spoonie, I'mma keep it real wit'chú man," Marcus began to explain. "I be needin' money true enuff, but I ain't no pack-workin' type of nigga."

"What, you think you too good to work a pack? How you think I got to where I'm at in the nation? We all had to start from somewhere!"

"Lord . . . You kno' I'a do whateva' for the team. Fuck a nigga up or whateva'. I jus' feel like I can do more than jus' work packs," Marcus explained, looking Spoonie directly in the eye with a serious expression.

13

Damn, this lil nigga bold and got balls of steel. I always knew he had it in him but he jus' put it out there front and center. Spoonie stood silent for a second as he thought to himself. "I kno' you different, that's why I got'a proposition for you . . . ," he said as he continued to smoke. "Smitty want me to open up shop on Twenty-first and Trumbull. He felt like it had cooled down ova' there since that murder happened last month . . ." Spoonie proceeded to pass Marcus the blunt before saying, "I need a stand up guy that I can trust to run the block. You kno', distribute the work, collect the money and report to me. Simple as that. You think you can handle that, big tyma'." Spoonie smiled at his sarcastic comment.

"Hell yeah, I can handle that. When we start?" Marcus asked anxiously as he passed the blunt back.

"We gon' start fresh on the first, which ain't nuttin' but a few days away so get'cha' mind right...It's time to start gettin' paid, lord," Spoonie said as they ended the conversation with the nation's handshake.

"Baby, don't trip, I'm on my way right now," Reggie spoke on the phone while walking up toward the two.

"Maaann, tell dat broad she gotta wait," Spoonie stated in a jokingly manner.

"Yeaaah, dat's Donisha lil thick ass. Boa, she don't kno' I'm fenna tear dat ass up!" He said with excitement.

"She kno' she got some good pussy to be so young. I'm still showin' her how to give good head, though," he bragged.

Spoonie had love for his homey, even though Reggie only bought weight from him and went on about his business. Spoonie knew if Reggie kept on chasing after younger girls, it would easily be his downfall.

"Regg, don't let dat broad get'chú caught up, lord. Go put dat shit up, then go get up wit' that hoe. Believe me, she ain't goin' nowhere," Spoonie gave his suggestion while slightly smiling.

"Awe Yeah, I feel you. She don't stay too far from where I'm takin' this shit so I'm cool."

"A'ight then, I'a holla' at'chú," Spoonie said as they shook up.

Weak-ass nigga. I'a take dat bitch from you wit' no problem. Jus' wait till I start gettin' to this money, Marcus silently directed his thoughts to Reggie as he stared him down until he got in his van and peeled out.

"Marcus . . . Marcus! Come'on, Jo, we all fenna ride up to Scatchell's and grab some'nt to eat, my treat!" Spoonie hollered out from where the crowd of lords stood.

Little did Marcus know this was the start of a new beginning for his life!

Chapter 3

Meanwhile back at home, Sylvia worked hard between two jobs and was trying to the best of her ability to keep her family intact. After a couple of weeks, Sylvia started noticing that Marcus was spending less time in the house. When he came in, it was only to change clothes and say hi and bye.

"Momma been lookin' for you," Chris informed Marcus as he walked up to their front porch.

"What she want?" Marcus asked nervously while attempting to straighten his face up from his high expression.

"I don't kno'. Go 'n' see," Chris said with a grin. He knew his brother was high by looking at him, and from Sylvia fussing around the house lately; Chris had a pretty good idea of what she wanted with him.

Marcus went into the house and ran straight for the bathroom. "Man, I wonder what the hell she wants," He mumbled to himself while splashing water on his face. "Whateva' it is, I jus' gotta deal wit' it."

As soon as Marcus opened the bathroom door, there she was standing outside the door waiting on him.

"I need to talk to you in the room, now!" She demanded with force.

"Okay," Marcus responded nervously.

On the walk to the room, Marcus's heart was beating through his chest. *I'm jus' gon' keep it real wit' her, let her kno' what's goin' on. Naw, fuck that, she might kick me out the crib wit' nowhere to go,* he rapidly thought to himself as they were approaching the bedroom.

"What's been goin' on with you?" Sylvia asked as she slammed the bedroom door behind them.

"What'chú mean?" Marcus countered while looking confused.

"What the hell you think I mean!" She began to raise her voice. "I can count on one hand how many times I saw you in the past couple weeks! I swear, if you—"

"Ma!" Marcus loudly interrupted. "You be at work all day and when I come in the house, you be sleep. You kno' I ain't gon' wake you up 'cause I know how tired you be from workin' so hard," he said with a sense of sympathy, attempting to soften his mother's words.

"Look, Marcus, I'mma tell you like this. If you out there doin' some shit you know damn well you ain't got no business doin', you might as well get cho' shit right now and find somewhere else to stay. Do you understand me!" she emphasized as she continued to snap.

She got her nerves to tell me some shit like this when the nigga she laying up wit' every night fuck wit' one of the biggest drug lords in the city, Marcus thought to himself for a split second without giving her a response while showing a disgusted expression as he stared his mother in her eyes

"Do you understand me?" Sylvia repeated forcefully.

"Yeah, Ma . . . I understand," Marcus replied with a cracked voice and a hurt expression upon his face.

From that moment on, there was no doubt in Marcus's mind that it was time for him to get out in the streets full fledged. When Marcus first opened up shop with Spoonie, he experienced the addictive adrenaline of making fast money. The excitement that filled his young mind led him to make the decision that the street life was going to be the career path for him until jail or death do him part!

"Yeah, who dis?" Marcus said as he spoke through the receiver of his mobile phone.

"Lord, I need'chú again!" the voice on the other end muttered out excitedly.

"Damn, already. I jus' left' you fifteen minutes ago," Marcus claimed as he recognized the voice being that of Lil G.

"You know' how this 'first of the month' shit go. How long you gon' be, Jo?"

"Gimme ten minutes."

"A'ight, I'mma be ova' Lisa crib. Call her phone when you make it out front."

"Bet," Marcus replied as they hung up from each other.

Even though Marcus wasn't working packs on the front line, his job was still challenging. It was his job to make sure each block that was in progress ran smoothly and never ran out of supplies. Spoonie let Marcus use one of his trap cars to get around so he could do the job successfully. After each thousand-dollar bundle was sold, Marcus would pick up the money, then supply the block with another "g-bundle." At the time, there were only two blocks that was in progress, Trumbull and Homan. These two blocks was right next to each other on the Twenty-first Strip. Both blocks had crack cocaine and heroin, but each block had different prices. Trumbull had the dimes (ten-dollar bags), and Homan had the dubs (twenty-dollar bags). Each block had its different clientele, from white people whom some were semi–truck drivers, to poor blacks that struggled to get "twos and fews." The first week of each month usually brought in double the money. If Marcus did his job successfully, he was paid a thousand dollars a week. He and his friends were making the same type of money, but theirs would come in quicker because they were on the front line selling packs.

"Aey, come'on out," Marcus called Lil G from his mobile phone.

"A'ight, here I come."

Marcus had just turned seventeen and didn't have a license to drive. Spoonie had a personal compartment built in the trap car for a stash spot so if he ever was pulled over, the police wouldn't be able to find the work.

"Man, I had to get me a quickie while I was waitin' on you, lord!" Lil G exclaimed as he got into the car and shook up with Marcus.

"I feel you, Jo; ole girl thick as hell!"

"Hell yeah!" Lil G agreed while gathering all the money he had on him. "Here go nine hundred and Shorty workin' on his last jab (pack). He should be through by the time we make it ova' there," he said as he counted the rest of the money in his hands, which was all his from the bundle he had finished working.

Marcus had keys to all stash houses that was operated by Spoonie. They had two to three different apartments that they switched up daily. The apartments were used to keep all the supplies for that day.

It had been nearly three months since the conversation between Marcus and his mother. Since then, Marcus made it obvious what his choice in life was when he eventually moved out the house. Not really having anywhere to go but to the block, Marcus was living from house to house with friends, until he got up with Peaches. Peaches was twenty-four years old and had three kids by three different baby daddies. Two of her kids' fathers were dead, and the other one was in prison with a forty-year sentence for kidnapping and first-degree murder. Despite Peaches having three kids and going through so much at such an early age, she wasn't too bad looking. Peaches was what they called a "red bone"—light skinned, stood about five foot six, nice thick thighs with very few stretch marks. She had nice round breasts with a little gut. Last but not least, she had an ass that all men in the 'hood would die to be next to. By looking at her, you could hardly tell she had three kids; Peaches was a typical ghetto queen: no job, on welfare, very little education, and a foul mouth. Peaches had a two-bedroom apartment in a sixteen-unit co-way building located on Twenty-first and St. Louis. The apartments in the building were all filled with drug addicts and underprivileged people who were on welfare. Marcus cared less about the living conditions as long as he was stationed a block or two from the spots that he was helping operate.

"Oooohhh, baby! Yeessss! Yeessss!" Peaches passionately moaned and groaned in the midst of Marcus sliding in and out of her. "That dick soooo gooood, baby!" she continued, obviously showing signs of satisfaction.

"How good?" Marcus said while in the heat of the moment as he fiercely pumped harder.

"Very!" she replied erotically.

"Awe yea!" Marcus teased as he continued to go hard.

As Marcus continued to penetrate inside Peaches, looking at her perfectly shaped round ass flap back and forth off his pelvic area made him want to bust all inside her, but he kept his composure and pulled out just in time. Peaches was used to dealing with big-time ballers, so sometimes she would question herself on why she was fucking with this young hustler; then she would always remember how mature Marcus was for his age and how well he put it down in the bedroom. Peaches had sex with several other men over the years, so it was surprising to her that he was the best she ever had sexually!

"Marcus, baby," She said while slowly licking Marcus's neck and passionately pecking his lips as he sat on the edge of the bed, rolling up a blunt after they were done having sex. "Yo' lil young ass kno' you be puttin' it down, don't you," she teased seductively.

"Well, ya kno', what can I say," he teased back at her before they were interrupted by the ringing of his phone. "Yeah," he answered.

"Aey, meet me downstairs in twenty minutes and bring that down wit'chú. I want you to ride somewhere wit' me."

"A'ight." Marcus said as they hung up from each other.

It was in the middle of a weekday, and Marcus knew that Spoonie was coming to pick up the money that was made off Trumbull and Homan from the morning shift. Usually Spoonie would come and leave after picking up the money if there weren't any problems on the block.

Marcus and Peaches were in the midst of going for a round two after they were done smoking. Ten minutes into her performing oral sex upon Marcus, they were once again interrupted by his phone.

"Hel . . . Hello?" Marcus hesitated from the warm sensation he was feeling as he answered his phone.

"Come'on out, Jo!" Spoonie said with a slight irritation in his tone.

"A'ight, here I come right now," Marcus replied frantically. Marcus didn't want to have Spoonie waiting outside too long, but he was reaching his peak from Peaches fiercely stroking his penis in an up-and-down motion while performing oral sex. Peaches knew Marcus was just about ready to explode from the way he was trembling and by his facial expressions, so she began stroking faster. Without giving a warning, Marcus let loose all inside her mouth. She accepted every drop of his natural juices and didn't complain about it like the professional that she was.

"Baby, I gotta ride out," Marcus said while gathering the money he had resting on the dresser along with his .9mm pistol that he kept on his waistline.

"Sweetie, leave me a few bags of weed and a couple dolla's. Since I know I'm prob'le ain't gon' see you no mo' for the rest of the day," she said in a sassy tone as she rolled her eyes.

Marcus pulled five dime bags of weed from his pocket and peeled off a hundred dollars in all fives and tens from his personal stash and handed it to her with no questions asked.

Hell, that's the least I can do being that I come and go out this ma'fucka as I please, Marcus thought to himself as a horn began to rapidly blow from outside.

"A'ight, I'm outta here. I'a holla' at'chú later," he said as he raced for the door.

"Yeah, this'll do for now, but he gon' have to start dropping more than this once he start makin' that real money wit' his fine ass," Peaches muttered to herself while watching Marcus out her window as she started rolling up a blunt.

"Damn nigga, I know that pussy good and believe me, I know," Spoonie stated with a slight smirk upon his face as if he was indicating that he had already ran through her. "But its business befo' pleasure; that's the only way we gon' make it out here on these cold streets of Chicago, Jo." Spoonie passed Marcus a blunt that was already sparked as he spoke.

Without knowing where they were headed, Marcus took the money out of a brown paper bag and started counting as they drove around the area, making their way down Trumbull and then down Homan, checking on how the block was moving.

"Here go ten thousand from the morning shift," Marcus began to explain while wrapping each five-thousand-dollar stack with a rubber band.

"Here go another five thousand from the start of the afternoon shift. I jus' dropped off a g-bundle on both blocks, so they should be cool for the next hour or two." After explaining, Marcus attempted to hand Spoonie the brown paper bag.

"Jus' put that in the glove compartment. I'll get it later."

"Where we on our way to?" Marcus asked.

"I'mma 'bout to meet that nigga Lil D ova' here on Cicero and Jackson. He been owing me some money for the longest. He called me earlier tellin' me that he had some'nt for me. So jus' in case he tryn'a get wrong I want a lil security wit' me, ya kno'," Spoonie spoke as they continued to smoke.

"You kno' it's whateva' wit' me. Jus' give me the tha' word. I stay ready!" Marcus exclaimed with much excitement as he tapped on his waistline, letting Spoonie know that he was strapped.

Spoonie could've got any one of the lords to ride with him, but he knew Marcus would let loose with no hesitation once he gave him the word.

"Yeah, where ya at?" Spoonie spoke into the receiver after making a phone call.

"I'm coming down Cicero now. I'll be on Jackson in one minute," said Lil D

"Hurry the fuck up, I ain't got all day!"

Lil D was a young dude that Spoonie sold pieces to. He wasn't moving major work, but he was doing enough to be riding in a clean Chevy Brougham sitting on 30s and Vogues with a banging sound system.

Spoonie pulled up at the gas station on Jackson and Cicero before seeing Lil D speeding as he made a quick turn into the gas station, banging his loud music in his money green Chevy that had a For Sale sign posted in the back window.

"How long you been waitin', lord?" Lil D asked as he raced over to the driver-side window of Spoonie car.

"Long enuff, so wassup, you got that paper you owe me?"

"Well, not all of it. How much I owe you, anyway?" Lil D asked confusedly.

"Don't fuckin' play wit' me! You kno' you owe me five stacks from that nina (nine ounces) that I fronted you. It's been damn near a month and this my first time hearin' from you." Spoonie was talking with an aggression in his tone that showed that he meant business.

"Awe," Lil D responded nervously. "I got'a couple thousand on me right now and I should have the rest for you later on when this nigga I know come buy my car."

"Shhiiit . . . I wouldn't mind havin' that clean muthafucka for myself," Marcus whispered out so that Spoonie only could hear him.

Marcus knew how to save money better than his friends, so after a couple of months of running the blocks for Spoonie and Smitty, he saved up a few thousand.

"How much you want for dat piece of shit!" Spoonie said jokingly, knowing that the car was clean as hell.

"Piece a shit . . . ?" Lil D asked but not really asking a question with a look of disbelief upon his face. "This ma'fucka got'a brand-new 350 engine under the 'hood. You see the paint job, flawless! I basically rebuilt this whole car from scratch. I gotta get at least forty-five hunit for it."

"How 'bout you gimme that ma'fucka and don't worry about the rest of the tab," Spoonie said while rubbing on the side of his face as if he was giving an offer that couldn't be refused.

"Hell naw . . . Jus' wait a couple hours and I'a have the rest of the bread, on tha' real, lord!" Lil D said, trying to be as respectable as possible, but little did he know he just pissed Spoonie off.

"What if I can't wait 'til later, if you get my drift," Spoonie said calmly as he glanced over at Marcus easing out his pistol from his waistline. "Jus' look at it like you payin' me interest for owing me so long," Spoonie muttered out with a devilish smirk on his face.

Lil D acted crazy, but he damn sure wasn't stupid by a long shot. He knew these guys meant business, and if he didn't cooperate, his ass would've been lying right where he stood. So Lil D politely dropped the money in Spoonie lap.

"You forgettin' somethin' ain't'chú; drop 'dem keys!"

"You want the car right now?" he asked with intimidation in his young eyes. "What about all my shit? Come-on Spoonie, man, I gotta clean this muthafucka out, and anyway you need the title and shit, right?" Lil D pleaded.

"You can pick all that shit up once you come on tha' block to drop off that title. Now if I have to repeat myself, you gon' have a big problem out here," Spoonie demanded in a low but aggressive tone.

Without any more questions asked, the keys were handed to Spoonie. "And please, don't have me knocking' on ya' momma door for the title to my car. I'm sure you don't want them type of problems, homey," Spoonie said smoothly as he handed the car keys to Marcus, pointing him in the direction to the car.

Spoonie drove behind Marcus as they skidded out the gas station, banging music out of both cars, leaving Lil D stuck with a sick expression on his face, like he lost the pride and joy of his life.

Chapter 4

Steve was on his side of town, which was not far from where he laid his head. He was well connected in his organization. I guess you could call him an OG because of all the work he put in for the CVL nation in the past years. Steve really didn't have it in him to lead a nation, so he became comfortable with just being Big C's silencer.

Big C was the son of a mob figure. His father was one of few blacks that were connected with the Italian mobsters of Chicago back in the seventies and eighties. Big C was more so of an extortionist type of kingpin. If there was anyone in the city of Chicago who claimed they were affiliated with the conservatives and they were getting a lot of money and didn't hold rank in the streets, he taxed them weekly. If for any reason they didn't pay the money, Big C would go shut them down and stop their cash flow.

Big C stood about six feet tall with a slight husky frame. He had a light-skinned complexion and always kept a serious expression upon his face. With his receding hairline and his dark-colored eyes with bags underneath, Big C looked to be well into his late forties but was only in his mid-thirties. Big C basically had Steve around him whenever he would rotate the streets. Steve was comfortable being Big C's shooter because he had love for him, but Steve wasn't getting nearly as much money as the young hustlers that had their own block; Big C made sure Steve was eating good and never wanted for anything.

Big C and Smitty did business together as bosses. You rarely saw these figures in the streets unless they called goals (meetings) amongst the nation when things weren't going well in the neighborhood or whenever they felt the opposition was trying to infiltrate.

In the meanwhile, Marcus was riding clean around the 'hood in his money green Chevy Brougham sitting on 30s and Vogues with four, twelve-inch kickers in the trunk, all sponsored by Lil D. Times when Marcus wasn't hustling, he would ride around the city and smoke. Most of the time he would end up on the far west side where his grandmother Emma lived. Emma stayed on Central and Division; over there were few vice lords and majority Four Corner Hustlas (another street organization).

The Foe's were a fairly new mob, but they were constantly growing in power and were spreading throughout the Chicago land. Marcus spent summers over at his grandmother's house as a youngster, so he knew how they got down. Marcus had little respect for the Foes once he moved to the Holy City area because he felt they were soft on that side of town. When Marcus would come through shining, guys over that way would hate on him hard. The Foes knew he was getting money, and they already were afraid of him—in other words, they didn't want any trouble.

A year had turned, and it was in the middle of the winter. This time of the season was called "grind season." The nice cars were put up, and guys usually hustled in all black Car hart coats and Timberland boots so they would be able to make it through the blistering cold. Snow damn near up to your knees and the temperature usually below zero. It didn't matter how cold it got or how much snow was on the ground, guys still had to stand out on the block to make sure the money came in right.

Everything was still going smoothly until the stick-up men started terrorizing certain blocks that was getting a lot of money at the time.

One day at the end of the night shift, Marcus made an unusual stop at Peaches' apartment on the corner of Twenty-first and St. Louis after collecting the night's earnings from both blocks (Homan and Trumbull). Marcus wasn't inside the apartment for more than fifteen minutes before coming back outside to approach his car and continue on his normal routine; what he didn't notice was two individuals parked directly behind his Chevy in an unknown vehicle with the windows extremely fogged up due to the cold weather, which made it impossible to see inside.

Before Marcus could make it all the way to his car, the passenger hopped out the parked car, followed by the driver.

"Don't'chú take another muthafuckin' step if you wanna live nigga!" one of the gunmen said while directing his pistol at Marcus. Marcus flinched and instinctively reached toward his waistline for his pistol, which he usually kept on him at all times, but not this particular time.

"Don't do nuttin' stupid. Put'cho' muthafuckin' hands up. I kno' you ain't tryn'a die ova' a lil money!" the other gunman exclaimed as they both quickly approached Marcus, putting both pistols close-up on him. While one of the stick-up men searched him down to see was he strapped and to take whatever he had on him, the other kept the gun to Marcus's face.

"Where the real money at? I kno' this ain't it. We kno' how y'all gettin' to 'dat money ova' here," the gunmen muttered out with a mischievous grin on his face as he pulled out roughly three to four hundred dollars out of Marcus's pockets.

"Man, that's all I got . . . !" Marcus said while trying to get a good look at the unfamiliar faces. "Now y'all betta' gone 'head 'n' take that shit 'fore it be too late for you pussies!"

"Bam!" Was the sound of one of the gunmen slapping Marcus across the forehead with the pistol.

"Get in and take us to where it's at then, nigga!" they said while forcing Marcus into his Chevy.

One of them kept the pistol to Marcus while the other tore through the inside of the car, searching for money and drugs. Little did Marcus know, these two individuals lurked and followed his every move—from the time he picked up Lil G from off Trumbull to collect the money from the night shift, all the way 'til he dropped Lil G off to where he needed to go. This routine went smoothly every night without any suspicion.

"Jackpot!" One of the gunmen blurted out with excitement after he forcefully broke open the glove compartment and saw the stacks of money.

"See, this all the fuck we wanted, right here . . . !" one of the gunmen said happily while stuffing the money inside his first down winter coat. "We even gon' let'cho' bitch ass live and let chú keep this piece of shit-ass car; but we'll hold on to these keys and this phone. Nice doing' bin'nis wit'chú, lord," Both assailants rushed out the car laughing after robbing Marcus of at least ten thousand dollars.

Instantly Marcus ran back up to Peaches' apartment to call Spoonie and inform him on what just had happened.

Knock! Knock! Knock! After the three loud knocks at the door, Peaches snapped as she answered, "Who the hell is it?"

"It's me baby, open the door'!"

"Why you ain't use yo' key. You know' these kids in here sleep!" Peaches fussed out while making her way to open up the door.

The moment Peaches cracked the door, she saw Marcus wiping blood from his forehead

"Oh my god! Baby, what happened!?" She asked dramatically with major concern while attempting to reach up at his head.

"I need to use the phone!" Marcus ignored her act of sympathy as he aggressively walked by her.

"The phone in the room, baby. I'mma get somethin' to clean up all that blood!" Peaches exclaimed as she quickly paced toward the bathroom.

While Marcus was on the phone, Peaches sat right next to him, attempting to clean the deep gash on his forehead while he explained the situation to Spoonie on the phone. If it was anyone else, Spoonie probably would've thought they were on bullshit, but since it was coming from Marcus, he knew it had to be true.

Spoonie was a stone-cold murderer, and he knew Marcus had it in him as well so he felt it was time for everyone to strap up.

"Yeah, who dis?" Smitty answered his cell phone.

"Chief, it's me. What's goin' on?" Spoonie spoke out.

"Shit, talk to me."

"Well, I told you about what happened the other day. I really wanna get to the bottom of this shit. A ma'fucka kno' betta' than to try us like that . . . You kno' what I mean?"

"You know' what to do. Come get wit' me so you can supply the 'hood wit' them tools . . . And If a muthafucka even look the wrong way, TOS they ass!" (Terminate on site) Smitty angrily demanded. "That's how we get to the bottom of shit. No ifs, ands, or buts about it!"

"I'm on my way to you, right now!" Spoonie assured

"You know where I'm at. I'll holla at chú in'a minute," Smitty said as they ended the call.

Marcus stood on Twenty-first a week straight with a TEC .9 with the strap across his shoulder to hold it up under his coat, waiting for any type of suspicion to come on the block.

Everything was cool until one cold winter night, an unfamiliar car crept through the block, and no one knew who was in the car due to the deep black tint that covered every window on the car. They finally pulled over as if they were trying to buy some dope.

"Yeah, who workin'?" Asked the driver as he pulled up to one of the Shorty lords, portraying to be a dope fiend.

"How many you need?" The Shorty that was working the pack asked anxiously without walking up to the car.

"Two jabs!" (Packs)

"A'ight. Pull over!" Shorty demanded while in the midst of jogging off to his hidden stash spot on the block.

Marcus was posted up in the gangway on the side of one of the resident houses on Homan where no one could see him as he watched the young hustler run to his stash spot excitedly to get the packs. Marcus knew something wasn't right with these dudes, but the Shorty was so anxious to finish up the bundle for he could get paid; he didn't care who the customers were that he was about to serve.

"Damn, Shorty, it took you long enuff. You gon' give me a play or what!" the driver said with his best dope-fiend expression.

"I can't give no plays right now . . . ," the Shorty said while approaching the parked car. "So you want this shit or not!" the Shorty said aggressively.

"We spendin' damn near two hunit and you can't work wit' us!"

"Hell naw!" the Shorty yelled with an attitude. "Now do y'all want this shit or not? You muthafuckas wastin' time. Them people already been hot as hell around here!" the Shorty said while nervously looking around for any detectives.

"Let me see it?" The driver asked.

"Let'chú see it?" Shorty said with a sense of disbelief. "Man, you playin' games, get the fuck on!" the Shorty said while in the midst of walking off.

"A'ight! A'ight, I got'chú . . . ," The driver replied, getting Shorty's attention as he began counting the money out. "You know how it is, some of you young niggaz be tryn'a take the money and run off 'n' shit."

"Not over here, homey. We all about that dolla' this way," the young hustler mentioned as he started reaching inside his pants for the packs. He never paid attention to the person in the backseat.

"Come-on, same time, man. I don't trust you!" the driver said anxiously.

As soon as the Shorty reached his arms and head inside the window with the work in hand, the person in the backseat had a chrome .357 Smith & Wesson pistol to the Shorty's face in a matter of seconds.

"Drop 'dat shit and empty everythang in 'nem pockets . . . ," the gunman in the backseat said in a low-pitched devilish tone. "If you make any false move, I'mma knock ya' shit back. Try me if you think I'm playin'!"

The Shorty knew dude with the gun meant business from the tone of his voice, so he dropped all the drugs in the driver's lap then dug into his pockets and grabbed all the money he had on him and did the same. Where Marcus was standing, he was able to witness everything that was going down. Marcus knew the Shorty was getting robbed from how he was digging into his pockets without taking his head out the window.

"Where the rest of it at!" The gunman said with death in his bloodshot red eyes, obviously scaring the living soul out of the Shorty lord.

"Dat's it, man, I swear! Jus' don't kill me, man, please!" the Shorty pleaded scarcely.

"Quit cryin' like a lil bitch! We gon' let'chu live but next time you might not be so lucky, you hear me, muthafucka!" The gunmen announced evil spiritedly.

"Yeah, yeah, I hear you, man!"

"Come-on, let's get the fuck outta here," The gunmen said as the driver proceeded to pull off with the Shorty's head still halfway in the car.

It was in the middle of one of the coldest winters in Chicago history, which meant ice and snow covered the streets. The stick-up men couldn't speed off without their car sliding and loosing control. Before they could react, they found themselves in the middle of an ambush.

Marcus came running from out the gangway firing the TEC .9 relentlessly at the car as it was slow to pull off. As he was unloading the fifty-shot extended clip, the driver panicked by pressing all the way down on the gas, causing the semi bald tires to burn rubber and spin out without the car being able to accelerate because of the slush and ice in the road. Marcus kept shooting the semi-automatic, shattering the back window and putting several bullet holes on the side of the car. By the time they were able to accelerate, the driver crashed into a parked car. Marcus then ran close-up on the car and aired the entire inside of the car out! I mean he made sure there wasn't a living soul left inside! Marcus escaped into the night, leaving two dead bodies in a running vehicle on Homan. This was the first of Marcus's killings, but it damn sure wouldn't be his last!

Chapter
5

Back home Sylvia didn't have to worry about working two jobs anymore; between Steve giving her money and Marcus sneaking in funds, she really had a chance to be a stay-home mother for Chris. By Marcus staying with different females and not being around the house much, Steve never really knew what nation Marcus was affiliated with, but he figured he was up to something.

The two bosses called a goal (meeting) in the spring of '92. The meeting was called to unite the two nations so they could make even more money and be more powerful than ever. At the meeting, Spoonie made it his business to make sure that Marcus and Smitty met face-to-face. Marcus had been putting in so much work for the past couple years, Spoonie felt like it was time for Marcus to move up in rankings. The meeting took place at Marcy Center, an open gym that's located on Sixteenth and Springfield.

The meeting began with Big C acknowledging everyone and reciting the nation's prayer.

"I wanna start by showing my appreciation to the high-ranked individuals for being responsible for their crews to be here. They know who they are. I also wanna give a moment of silence for all the fallen soldiers we had ova' the years. Their lives will never be forgotten . . . As I start with the opening prayer, I advise everybody to 'palms up' and bow your heads," Big C demanded. Everyone followed suit.

"In the name of Allah, most gracious, most merciful, praises be to Allah, the Cherisher and Sustainer of the world's, most gracious, most merciful, the Master of the day of judgment, thee do we worship and thine aid

we seek. Show us the straight way, the way of those on whom thou has bestowed thy grace those portion is wrath and who go not astray . . . Amen." After reciting the opening prayer, Big C chanted the word, "Almighty!"

"Almighty!!!" The crowd of about fifteen hundred lords roared back.

Big C put out suggestions and spoke his peace. Smitty took the podium next; he accepted the suggestions Big C presented, and he gave some of his own. Everyone agreed on the terms that were given out. Now came the part of the meeting where the bosses chose a special someone to get blessed with some juice! Spoonie had already "spit a bug" in Smitty ear about Marcus being that dude.

At the end of every meeting, the bosses and other high officials would stand in a circle to discuss the facts of the meeting. In this circle stood Big C, Smitty, Steve, a couple of their bodyguards, and a few other high-ranked figures.

Spoonie headed toward the circle with Marcus behind him. As Spoonie and Marcus made it to the circle, Steve and Marcus locked eyes with each other immediately! The expressions on their faces were so intense; you would've thought they were getting ready for a twelve-round brawl!

Marcus had been blessed with three-star elite status at the age of nineteen, one of the youngest elites in the nation. Marcus was blessed differently than any other three-star elite. Instead of being in control of an area that was already in progress, he had the opportunity to operate his own block. Marcus already had in mind what land he wanted to work on and who he needed on his personal team.

Marcus's block was located on Avers and Cermak, sort of in the middle of lands, the Twenty-first Strip and the Sixteenth area. Marcus didn't believe in having new faces around him, so he had his same childhood friends as his crew members: Mikey, Pee Wee, JR, Lil G, and Marlin.

Mikey was one person everyone would love to have on their team. He was the silencer of the crew and also the oldest, so he understood the "ends and outs" of the game. Mikey stood about five foot nine and sported a Low Top Fade. He wasn't the most attractive person in the world due to his bad case of acne that covered his face. What attracted women to Mikey was his distinctively deep voice and his groggy-style type of laugh.

Pee Wee on the other hand was the wild one out the crew. All of Marcus's guys had the heart to put in work at any given time, but Pee Wee just didn't give a fuck. Whoever Marcus needed out the way, Pee Wee would do it in a heartbeat! Even if Marcus decided to give someone a pass, Pee Wee would still take them out just to stop any future problems with that person. Pee Wee was as black as charcoal and had braids straight to the back. Pee Wee didn't care too much about fashion as much as the others. He was satisfied with a pair of Dickies khaki pants with the button-up shirt to match and whatever new pair of Jordan's that came out. Majority of his money went to buying new guns and weed.

Lil G and Mikey were actually blood cousins. They were always together, and they went on most of their missions together; they had similar ways.

Lil G stood six feet three inches tall with a husky type of build, not too muscular and not too chubby. With his short wavy hairstyle and a baby face that attracted all the young ladies, he was more of a ladies' man than his cousin Mikey.

JR was the so-called book smart one out the crew; he actually graduated from high school with average grades and went on to take business management classes at Malcolm X Junior College for one year. JR was the type that didn't do unnecessary hanging out. If there weren't any business to be handled in the streets, JR would usually be in the house on standby. With his five-foot-nine skinny frame and his bald head with a full connected beard and mustache, JR wasn't the gigolo type of guy like the rest of the crew. He actually had a main girl he was living with whom he planned on marrying and adding on more kids to the two they already had. JR was settled down at the early age of twenty, but he was still very much involved in the street life.

Marlin was the hustler; I mean, rain, sleet, hail, snow, Marlin stayed on the block, grinding. Marlin was short with a light brown complexion. He always dressed in grimy clothes because he was always on the block. But when it came time to dress, he would splurge and buy some of the most expensive gear. When it came time to play, he would definitely dress to impress. Marcus treated all his guys equally but always assigned them to different daily tasks.

In the meanwhile, Christopher was pursuing his basketball career. He was starting at the point guard position on the seventh—and eighth-grade team while only being in the sixth grade. Chris stood about five foot five but could shoot three-pointers with the best of them.

Christopher's grades were beginning to fall because of him being more focused on basketball and less on his schoolwork.

"Christopher . . . Christopher!" Sister Mary Ellen yelled out for Chris's attention, his sixth-grade history teacher.

"Huuuh . . . what, I ain't sleep," Chris quickly responded while lifting his head up from being in a deep sleep.

"Christopher, I need to have a serious talk with you after class!"

"Shhit," Chris muttered in a hushed tone.

"What was that?"

"Nuttin', I ain't say nothin'," Chris replied with a slight attitude. Out of all his sixth-grade teachers, Sister Mary Ellen wasn't the one to fool around with. Her white hair and wrinkled-up skin made her look very scary.

"All right, class, I need the essay completed by Friday, no later! Any papers turned in after Friday will automatically receive a failing grade!" she stated with emphasis as the bell rang for changing periods.

"Christopher! Where do you think you're going? I need to have a word with you!" she demanded while witnessing Chris trying to slip out with the rest of his classmates.

"Yes," Chris answered with a slow drag.

"What's been going on with you lately?" she asked with a concerned expression upon her face.

"What'chú mean?" Chris countered while looking confused.

"What I mean is . . . ," She paused in between her statement. "For the past two weeks you've either been late with your assignments or just not turning them in, and on your past three tests you received lower than a 70 percent on each of them. You know what this means, right?" She asked

"No," Chris answered, hoping she wasn't about to say what he was thinking.

"No . . . ?" She questioned his answer in disbelief as she gave a sarcastic grin. "You are kidding me, right?

"No, I'm not kiddin'. What does it mean?" Chris said with more seriousness in an irritable tone.

"It means, as of today you are failing my history class. Now do you understand, mister?"

"Yeah," Chris answered with disappointment written all over his face.

"Now to my understanding you need at least a C average in order to be eligible for next week's game, correct?"

"Yes."

"Now what's wrong with this picture?"

"What'chú mean?"

"I just told you that you're failing my class. I have to turn in your progress report to the coach by the end of the week. That's not enough time for you to bring your grades up from an F all the way to a C average or better. You might have to play the sidelines this week and possibly the rest of the season," she explained.

Chris stood there looking disappointed as his teacher broke the bad news to him.

"There ain't nuttin' I can do?" Chris pleaded.

"Nope. At least not before the upcoming game. Now if you're willing to put forth an effort to raise your grade, I can assign you some extra assignments. Not only that, you still would have to keep up with our everyday tasks. You'll have to pass every test from here on out with at least a B average or better, and the essay that's due Friday will have to be superb!" she instructed while looking Chris directly in the eyes. "Do you think you will be able to handle that?"

"Yes . . . !" Chris answered desperately. "I got no other choice."

"I don't know if you're thinking realistically, but I guess it's worth a try. Now if somehow you pull this off, you'll be eligible to play in the play-offs three weeks from now."

"Come-on wit' it, I can handle it," Chris said with confidence.

"All right, see me at the end of the day and I'll have your assignments ready for you."

As Chris was leaving out the classroom, he was shaking his head in disbelief at all the extra work he had ahead of him. He knew it would be damn near impossible to make up past assignments and still maintain a passing grade in the rest of his classes. As he continued to walk down the hallway to his next class with his head down, a voice came from behind him that distracted him from his train of thoughts.

"Chris!" a loud voice of a young lady yelled. Chris picked his head up and looked back to see that it was Bridget Adams calling him. Bridget was Chris's girlfriend; she was a grade higher than Chris.

"Wassup?" he responded in a low, depressing tone.

"What'chú don' did now? Everybody told me you got in trouble," Bridget said as she walked up.

"I ain't get in any trouble. And what'chú doin' in the hallway after the bell, anyway?"

"I got'a hall pass to go to the washroom," she replied. "But this isn't 'bout me right now, this is about you," she continued.

"Maaann, Sister Mary Ellen trippin' 'n' shit, talkin' 'bout if I don't pick my grades up I ain't gon' be able to play for the rest of the season, including the play-offs," Chris explained.

"Are you serious?"

"Hell yeah . . . !" He said harshly with a frown. "She gets on my damn nerves. Now I don't know what I'mma do. I mean, she givin' me some extra work to do but I know I ain't gon' be able to do all that shit!"

"Well, baby, you know I will help you out with whatever you need."

"I'm sho'll gon' need it," Chris responded with a sympathetic expression.

"I'll talk to you more about it later. Gimme a hug and a kiss before I go," she requested while approaching Chris with open arms.

"Can I go in 'nere wit'chú?" Chris mentioned as they sneaked a hug and a kiss without the teachers noticing them.

"No!" Bridget said humorously while seductively walking away.

St. Angela was undefeated, and they also were the favorite to win the championship. A big part of their success came from Chris's production on the court, averaging twenty-five points and ten assists per game. It was safe to say that without Chris's presence, St. Angela would be doomed come play-off time.

Bridget was an honor student and very mature for her age. She stood a couple of inches taller than Chris. Dark skinned with full juicy lips and long jet-black hair. Bridget had a body of a woman in her twenties, and she was only in junior high. All her body parts were fully grown, and she was only thirteen years old!

Bridget made it her business to help Chris out with his homework. She also tried stopping him from fooling around in the classrooms and in the hallways during passing periods but to no avail.

After a couple of weeks of consistent working and with the help of Bridget, Chris was able to raise his GPA up to a C, which was good enough for his eligibility for St. Angela's first play-off game that was coming up the following week.

Chapter 6

Since the meeting, Steve had been sending word through the streets for Marcus to get in touch with him. Ever since Marcus moved up in rank and became a boss over his own crew under the IVL nation, he made it difficult for certain individuals to get up with him.

"Aey, Pee Wee . . . !" Steve hollered out his car window while pulling up next to a parked car on Avers one weekday afternoon. "Let me holla at'chú for a minute."

"Hold on y'all, let me see what he want," Pee Wee stated in a low tone as he walked off from the crowd of guys that surrounded him on the block. "Wassup, Unc, what's goin' on?" Pee Wee acknowledged Steve as he approached the driver's side of the car, resting his arms on the car window seal.

"I can't call it, you been a'ight?" Steve asked as he reached his hand out to give Pee Wee five.

"Aw yeah, I'm straight. Jus' out here tryn'a make it happen."

"Yeah, I hear dat. How it's been doing over here so far?" Steve asked curiously, showing signs of suspicion in his expression.

"You know we jus' jumped down a week ago but I can tell its gon' pick up soon."

"Aw yeah," Steve replied, raising both eyebrows.

"Hell yeah! Especially with this new batch of dope we jus' put out here today. They say that shit'a bomb! Look across the street at Hotrod ass," Pee Wee said as he lifted up from off the car to point across the street.

"He jus' bought a blow from us not too long ago."

"Gaaaddamn!" They both said at the same time with excitement as they watched one of the neighborhood hypes stopped in his own tracks while leaning all the way over into a deep nod, head damn near reaching his crouch area, but somehow he managed not to fall over.

"Hotrod been getting high for a long time and I ain't seen him that fucked up in'a while," Steve claimed as he grinned while still looking back at Hotrod leaned over.

"When them dope fiends react like that, that's when you know you got'a bomb, Jack!" Steve said as he and Pee Wee shared a laugh.

"I told you, Unc!" Pee Wee exclaimed

"Aey, where Marcus at, man?" Steve asked after a couple more minutes of staring and laughing at Hotrod snapping in and out of a deep nod.

"I ain't seen him since I lef' him earlier this morning," Pee Wee claimed.

"Did you tell'em I been tryn'a get up wit'em?"

"Yeah, I told him. He said he was gon' get wit'chú," Pee Wee said. "He ain't at the house?" Pee Wee asked, already knowing Marcus wasn't there.

"Nawl. Me or his momma ain't seen him. Every time I call that number you gave me I never got an answer. That's the only number you got on him?" Steve asked

"Yep, that's it."

"Well, when you see him later make sho' you tell'em to get up wit' me, it's real important!"

"A'ight, I got'chú."

"Don't forget!" Steve said with emphasis.

"I got'chú, Unc. I ain't gon' forget," Pee Wee assured him before shaking up with Steve and heading back toward the crowd.

"He can forget about it." Pee Wee mumbled to himself on his walk back.

Chris was so excited about being eligible to participate in St. Angela's first play-off game that he wanted everyone to be there, especially Marcus.

"Yeah, who dis?" Marcus asked as he answered his cell phone.

"This yo' lil brotha', wassup!" Chris spoke excitedly. "I'm surprised you answered the phone."

"You the only one in the family that got this number so if this would've been anybody else, I was gon' whoop ya' ass 'cause I told you not to give this number out to nobody!" Marcus joked aggressively with his little brother.

Marcus enjoyed conversing with Chris every chance that he got. This particular day Marcus was rotating around the neighborhood scoping things out while smoking a blunt to himself. This was how he relaxed and thought about his next move. Marcus was a thinker but still had so much to learn about the life he was leading.

"Where you at?" Chris asked.

"Don't worry 'bout it. What the hell you want, anyway?"

"Damn, I jus' can't call my big bra' to see wasssup?"

"Hell naw! Now tell me whatchú want 'fore I hang up on yo' ass," Marcus said in the midst of laughing through the receiver. Marcus and his little brother always talked shit to each other for fun. Everyone in the family and that was close to the family knew how much love Marcus had for his younger sibling, but majority of the time they showed tough love.

"Man, I was jus' calling' to let'chú know about my game this weekend. You gon' be there, right?" Chris demanded

"I don't know, I might have some'nt to do, Jo," Marcus claimed.

"Let'chú not be there, me and you gon' fight, dude!"

"I don't know why you want me to see you stank up the gym, anyway!" Marcus said, but knowing Chris was the best player St. Angela had, even though he was the youngest on the team. Marcus knew if Chris continued to stay focused on basketball that he would have a promising career ahead of him.

"Yeah, you'a luv that. Man, is you coming' or not?"

"Where it's gon' be at?"

"At the Merrilac House on Jackson, right off California. The game start at two o'clock but I advise you to get their earlier 'cause it's gon' be packed wit' people there to see me," Chris exaggerated in a boasting manner, but in all actuality, Chris was a crowd pleaser.

"Yeah, I guess I'd be there. If y'all don't win I'mma beat'cho' ass for wasting my time! Who y'all playin', anyway?"

"Resurrection," Chris answered.

"Aw yeah . . . ," Marcus said in between puffs of smoke. "They gon' blow y'all ass out. Dem boys be ballin'," Marcus teased.

"You crazy as hell!" Chris replied.

"A'ight, Jo, let me get my ass off this phone. I'll holla' at'chú later."

"Wait . . . !" Chris yelled out anxiously. "You comin' through here later on? I need a few dolla's."

"I ain't'cho' daddy; Speaking of dude, where he at?"

"I don't know I ain't seen him today."

"A'ight, man, I'll be through there."

"A'ight," Chris responded as they hung up the phone from each other.

Chris got off the phone feeling good inside. It always excited him when he knew his brother was coming around. Since Marcus moved out the house, Chris wasn't able to see him as much.

The play-off game fell on a Saturday afternoon, and majority of Chris's family was there; Sylvia, Grandma Emma, and Steve all sat next to each other on the bleachers while watching St. Angela struggle throughout the first quarter.

"I told Chris about playing' so damn soft . . . !" Steve stated intensely. "He needs to attack the basket and quit settling for the outside shot!" he continued to complain while talking to Sylvia.

"Well you know, sweetie, it takes time for him to get into a groove. He'll get it together. Don't be so hard on'em," Sylvia replied, being sympathetic toward her son's poor play-off performance.

"Baby, you don't understand. If Chris expects to play successfully on that next level, he's gonna have to be more aggressive and play with more heart and passion!" Steve expressed himself with a slight aggression.

"He's only in the sixth grade, Steve . . . !" She responded, showing a sign of irritation in her tone of voice. "I'm sure he'll get it together in due time. Hell, if you ask me he's doing damn good to be a starter on the eighth-grade team. Two levels higher! Anyway, I'm not about to go there with you."

Steve sat there shaking his head with anger. By Steve's intensity level, it was obvious that he wanted nothing more than to see Chris become more successful and make it further than he did in the profession.

"Baby, you seen Marcus around here in the crowd anywhere? Chris told me that he promised to show up," Sylvia asked as she glanced around the packed gym.

"Naw, baby, I ain't seen 'em. You kno' he prob'le to busy for some'nt like this," Steve responded sarcastically.

"Well, Momma been asking about him so I was just hoping he showed up," Sylvia explained in a sorrowful manner.

Even though Steve acted nonchalant about Marcus's temporary absence, he knew this would be the best time to catch up with him being that he had been unsuccessful in reaching him in the streets.

It was the end of the third quarter. The packed crowd was in frenzy from St. Angela going on a 10-0 run to cut a fifteen-point deficit down to a five-point game.

Marcus finally strolled in the gym with a few of his crew members behind him; all of them dressed in Girbaud outfits with $700 leather Pellé Pellé jackets on. Their clothes reeked with Marijuana smells, and all their eyes were low.

"Damn, this muthafucka packed, ain't it?" Marcus stated as they all took post and examined the gymnasium.

"Hell yeah! You'a think Jordan or somebody was playing in this bitch!" Mikey replied.

"Aey, y'all help me find my people. I know' they around here somewhere," Marcus said while looking around the gym.

"Aey Jo, ain't dat Steve sitting' right there," Lil G alarmed Marcus while pointing in their direction.

"Where?"

"Right there! Matter of fact, yo' ole girl sittin' next to'em," Lil G spoke out while pointing through the crowds to assure Marcus on where his people were seated.

"Hell yeah, that's them . . . There go my granny too. Damn, I ain't tryn'a be all in her face 'n' shit while I'm high," Marcus said with a paranoid smile on his face.

"Well, I don't know about y'all but I'm goanna get on some of these older bitches that I see in the crowd, ya dig!" Mikey said as he walked off from the two.

Marcus staggered his way through the crowd to where his family was stationed.

"Hey Ma!" Marcus greeted his mother with a smile but hugged his grandmother so sincerely it seemed that he didn't want to let her go. Marcus sat down next to Grandma Emma and conversed with her without acknowledging Steve at all.

"Haaaeeeyy, babe . . . !" she reacted dramatically at Marcus's actions. "You jus' forgot about ole Granny, huh?"

"Nah, Granny, it ain't like that," Marcus replied while in the midst of kissing her on the cheek. "I jus' been tryn'a get myself together," Marcus finished explaining as they settled in to the bleacher.

"Your mother told me you haven't been staying at the house lately, everything all right?" she asked while staring directly in Marcus's eyes and holding on to his hand with a tight grip.

"Yes, ma'am, everything's cool. I jus' been staying' wit' my lady friend until I find my own place," Marcus said, trying to straighten his face from a high expression.

"You know Granny be worried about you. My door is always open if you need somewhere to stay, you hear me?" Grandma Emma forcefully assured.

"Yes, ma'am, I know," he answered sincerely.

"And why your eyes so red? You sick or something', shuga'?" she asked curiously while gently rubbing the side of Marcus's face.

"Nah, Granny, I'm just a little tired," Marcus retorted with a high grin upon his face.

"Ummm hmmm! You need to leave them tweeds alone or whatever y'all young folks call y'all self smoking these days. You know Granny far from crazy," Grandma Emma said humorously before they both shared a laugh. They focused back on the game after the crowd reacted to a three-point shot Chris knocked down to tie the game with three minutes left on the clock in the fourth quarter.

At this point Marcus made it very obvious that he had been ignoring Steve's quest to reach out to him.

The game was coming to an end, and Chris had been struggling throughout the entire game with only fourteen points and three assist. It came down to ten seconds left on the clock, and St. Angela was down two points.

"Put the ball in Chris's hands, coach!" Marcus yelled across the court as St. Angela came out of a time-out with the possession. The defense on the other team was so aggressive; they forced St. Angela to call their last time-out. The entire packed gym was so intense and quiet you could've heard a pen drop.

After St. Angela came out of the time-out, Resurrection already had a pretty good idea whose direction St. Angela were going in. After having trouble inbounding the ball, Chris eventually got it in his hands.

"Pick! Pick!" Chris called out a pick-and-roll that got him open for a three-point field goal.

"Got'em!" Chris yelled out as he released the shot as if he already made the basket. Sure enough the shot went in, hitting nothing but net!

"Yes! Yes!" Marcus hollered out wildly with excitement while running onto the court, being the first person to grab hold of Chris, followed by the rest of his teammates. St. Angela ended up winning the game by one point, and the gym went up in a roar!

Once the court became really crowded with everyone celebrating, Marcus attempted to slip out the crowd without anyone noticing. As soon as Marcus made his way to the exit, he was met by Steve. At that point there was no avoiding him.

"Was sup man . . . ?" Steve asked aggressively. "Why you ain't been returning none of my calls?"

Marcus stood there emotionlessly with wandering eyes, avoiding all eye contact with Steve. "I been busy," Marcus simply replied, nonchalantly.

"Too busy for family?" Steve asked vigorously.

"Family?" Marcus responded with an estranged expression. "What family you talking about?"

"Awe, I hope you don't think them guys you be wit' is yo' family 'cause they don't give a fuck—"

"Look, man," Marcus cut Steve off from making his statement. "What this shit all about?"

"Marcus, do you even know whatchú got'cha'self into?"

In the back of Marcus's mind, he wondered why all of sudden Steve acted as if he cared about his well-being.

"Look, Steve . . . !" Marcus said firmly while looking Steve directly face-to-face. "I'm grown. I can take care of myself, a'ight!"

As the gymnasium began clearing out, the hallways became flooded with noisy people, from young kids jumping around reenacting the dramatics of the game, to security trying to get everyone to cooperate and exit safely.

"Aey, lord, you seen how Chris was fuckin'nem up out there . . . !" Lil G said with much excitement as he and Mikey walked up to approach Marcus, rudely interrupting him and Steve's conversation. "Dat lil nigga raw as hell!"

"Was sup, Unc?" Mikey greeted Steve with a handshake.

"Yeah, wassup, y'all straight?" Steve asked halfheartedly.

"Yeah, we good . . . !" Marcus interrupted. "Come-on y'all, let's get up outta here. We got shit to do."

Marcus and his guys proceeded to leave out the building before Steve yelled out, "Aey, Marcus . . . !"

"What!" Marcus countered back angrily while still walking with his back turned.

"We need to finish talking' . . . !" Steve demanded.

"You know' where to find me," Marcus replied as he continued to walk.

"Where?"

"On tha block!" Marcus answered by glancing back with a slight smirk before walking through the exit doors.

St. Angela ended up losing in the second round of the tournament on the road against an underrated all-white St. Benedict Catholic School. St. Angela underestimated the other team and got "shot out" the gym!

Chapter 7

Marcus had his block pumping with crack, heroin, and something didn't too many hustlers had in the 'hood at the time, some good mid-grain weed. Guys had to drive outside the neighborhood to get good weed. Smitty weren't too concerned about Marcus having weed on the block as long as Marcus continued to get his supply of cocaine and heroin from him.

Marcus stumbled across his own connect to supply the weed, a Mexican by the name of Puncho. Puncho was a fairly frail guy who stood about five foot three. He sported a ball head and had a few tattoos of teardrops falling from his eyes, which usually meant that they were affiliated and had put in a lot of work for the love of their gang. Puncho was a representative of the Latin Kings; their sets were across the railroad tracks along Twenty-Sixth Street. The tracks separated the blacks from the Hispanics.

Before becoming acquainted, Marcus and Puncho very first encounter occurred on an unusually warm eighty-degree sunny October afternoon. While driving down Cermak, Marcus decided to stop at Diaz Muffler Shop, located on Cermak and Kedzie, deep in the Hispanic neighborhood. Marcus was having trouble with his Chevy's exhaust pipes and needed a new muffler. Marcus was familiar with the shop because most big-timers from the 'hood would go there if they need major work done to their cars. Marcus knew he was on unfamiliar territory but wasn't too worried due to the fact he had his personal bodyguard on him, nina ross.

"Aey, where Hernandez at?" Marcus asked one of the Mexican workers as he pulled into one of the open garage doors at the muffler shop.

"O ye, Hernandez, hay un mayate aqui que te quiere, que bajes," the Mexican hollered out, as his manager proceeded down the stairs.

"Que pasa, primo," Hernandez said while coming down the stairs to approach Marcus.

"Come-on, primo, speak English, bro!" Marcus said as he smiled while shaking hands with Hernandez. "I need some work done to my baby, primo."

"Not this thing of beauty," Hernandez replied. "What's wrong with it?"

"The muffler scrapes the ground every time I hit a bump and I need some new dual pipes so this muthafucka can get up, you kno' what I'm saying', bro!" Marcus explained excitedly, while rubbing both hands together. They both walked over to the Chevy Brougham to examine the problem.

As Marcus and Hernandez continued to converse, they both were interrupted by a '69 two-door candy-apple red drop-top Chevy Impala with gold day tons that had graphics of the character Chucky stabbing a knife through the paint from the driver's side door to the back end of the car. The sound system was banging so hard that the garage doors were rattling. All you heard was the lyrics of Dr. Dre featuring Snoop Dogg's Deep Cover soundtrack.

"Yeeaahh and ya' don't stop 'cause it's 187 on a undercover cop . . ." was blasting through the four twelve-inch punch speakers in the Impala.

Marcus and Hernandez turned their attention toward the Impala that was four deep with young Latin Kings.

Fuck, I hope these fools don't start trippin', Marcus thought to himself.

The young LKs adjusted the volume to their loud music as they settled into the shop. "Aey, holmes, check out that mayaté standing over there," the LK in the backseat whispered as he tapped the driver on the shoulder. "I say we move on'em, essé."

"Puncho, my main man! What can I help you with today?" Hernandez asked with fear in his eyes, not knowing what Puncho and his wild crew was up to.

Puncho . . . Marcus thought to himself. *Damn that name sounds familiar.*

Marcus stood about five feet from the car alongside Hernandez; Marcus eyed each one of the LKs down with a cold stare in his eyes as they exited the Impala.

"I jus' stopped by to visit an ole friend . . . ," Puncho said with a stale expression, with suspicion in his eyes. "Where's Diaz?"

"Ohhh . . . I . . . I don't know, primó. I haven't seen him in'a while," Hernandez stuttered out while performing nervous hand gestures as he explained.

Marcus stood across from Puncho, looking slightly puzzled as he listened to them converse. Marcus kept his hands close to his waistline while glancing back and forth at Puncho and his guys.

"Somethin' tellin' me that your boss is avoiding me. I hope that isn't the case 'cause if so . . ." Punchó shook his head from left to right while making a ticking sound from his mouth. "God bless," he finished his statement before flaming up a Newport. "Wassup, bro . . . ?" Punchó greeted Marcus suspiciously while exhaling a breath of nicotine smoke. "Where you from, holmes?"

Marcus stood there for a few seconds, keeping his eyes focused on the LKs and Puncho at the same time before saying, "I'm from around here . . . !" Marcus replied argumentatively, "Wassup, it's a problem?"

"You a GD, holmes?" Puncho asked as he flicked the half-smoked cigarette to the ground. The other three LKs started easing their way closer to the conversation.

"Hell naw . . . !" Marcus replied vigorously. "I'mma vice lord from out the Holy City!" His belligerent facial expression showed that he was beginning to feel agitated about the whole situation.

Marcus knew if he was a GD, guns would've been drawn immediately; Latin Kings and GDs don't coincide at all in the city.

By Marcus being affiliated and a young black male in the wrong 'hood, there was a chance that it still could go down.

"Dig man, I ain't ova' here to disrespect y'all set. I'm well aware of where the fuck I'm at. I'm strictly ova' here to get my car checked out," Marcus explained

"This yo' Chevy right here, holmes?" Puncho asked, walking toward the front of the Brougham while checking it out.

"Yeah, that's me," Marcus answered while still feeling uneasy about the situation, not knowing what the esse's next move was going to be.

"Your job must pay you well?" Puncho asked sarcastically, knowing Marcus didn't fit the profile of the working type.

"It pays a'ight," Marcus replied, matching his mockery.

Marcus and Puncho continued to converse. In the midst of them talking, they found out that they both briefly attended Farragut High School, located a few blocks from Diaz muffler shop in the heart of the esse's territory. Majority of blacks attended the school because it was one of the only high schools in the district. That's where Marcus remembered hearing the name Punchó.

Back then, young blacks that were affiliated had to fight different Mexicans everyday on their way to and from school. Puncho was the leader over every Latin King that attended Farragut at the time.

A couple of months after clashing heads with Puncho at Diaz muffler shop, Marcus had started getting pounds of weed from Puncho off consignment.

Marcus had a master plan in progress. All the hard drugs were sold in the alley and the weed on the front. Marcus only had ole-school addicts working the packs in the alley because he knew it would be a good cap off for when the detectives swerved through. Another thing, Marcus didn't have to pay the workers much; a blow to wake them up and another one when their shift ended, they would work all day and all night, happily. Marcus had the young lords on the front of the block working all the weed jabs.

It was the spring of '93, and the weather was starting to break. The weed was selling better than Marcus expected, and it attracted a lot of girls and young guys to the block.

Buummp! Buummmp! One of the young lords from the neighborhood blew his horn at Marcus and Marlin as they stood on Avers. "Wudd'up, lord?" the young dude hollered out the car window as he sped through the block in what looked to be a stolen vehicle.

"That lil dude a live wire!" Marcus said to Marlin while throwing up the deuce at the Shorty.

"Hell yeah! Shorty, twelve goin' on twenty 'n' shit!" Marlin smiled as they both stood there looking at the car until it got out of eyesight.

"It's startin' to feel good outside, ain't it?" Marcus said, rubbing both hands together excitedly.

"Hell yeah . . . ," Marlin replied while grabbing hold to his crouch area. "And that weed startin' to pick up too."

"I see!" Marcus said surprisingly. "Jus' last week we was only doin' 'bout five to six jabs a day. Now a ma'fucka doin' ten to fifteen jabs. Shhiiit, since I been standin' here I seen three different cars ride up and bought whole jabs!"

"That's because it's gettin' hot; everybody wonna smoke and hit blocks."

It was a mid-seventy-degree weekend day, the type of day where you could hear the leaves moving on the trees from the blowing of the mild wind. The sky was a bluish orange type of setting due to the sunset. It was late in the afternoon going into evening time, and Avers Street was packed with people—kids running back and forth to the snowball stand, riding their bikes up and down the sidewalks; young boys wrestling with each other in the half-burned-out grass; different people walking and driving up, buying weed from the Shorty's that was working. All this traffic was happening on the front of the block while the real money was being made in the back alley.

"Hey, y'all!" a group of females walking down Avers hollered from across the street at Marcus and Marlin.

Marcus didn't get a chance to speak before Marlin shouted, "Ke-ke! Slow up! I need to holla' at'chú!" Marlin began making his way across the street toward the five-girl group. "I gotta get up wit' her for the night, for real, lord," he mentioned to Marcus in a low tone while in the midst of crossing the street.

"Damn, Marcus! You can't speak now . . . ," Donisha shouted in a sarcastic tone from the other side of the street. "Don't be ova' there actin' funny 'n' shit!"

"Girl ain't nobody actin' funny!" Marcus responded. "Wassup wit'chú?"

"Shhiiit," Donisha replied while volunteering her way toward Marcus's presence without an invite.

Since Marcus started making a lot of money, his dress code became spectacular. This particular day he wasn't dressed to impress, but his swagger basically brought out whatever he wore. He stood on the block wearing a pair of Brand X Girbaud jeans with a white Girbaud T-shirt with different writings on it and some all-white Diadora sneakers. This was the type of gear that attracted 'hood girls, especially if they knew that there was money behind a certain individual.

"*I was jus' speaking', that don't mean bring yo' ass ova' here . . . ,*" Marcus mumbled to himself. "*That ass is looking' good in dem jeans, tho'.*" Marcus nonchalantly checked Donisha out from head to toe as she crossed the street.

Marcus always saw Donisha and her crew when he would ride down Twenty-first, but the most he would do nowadays was blow the horn and keep it moving.

"Wassup?" Donisha greeted him in a quarrelsome but feminine tone as she slightly pushed Marcus in the chest area.

"Shhiit. You wassup," Marcus retorted with a smirk.

"I can't tell. The only time I see you now is when you flying pass the block bangin' that loud-ass music. You be actin' like you ain't got time to stop and holla' at a bitch no mo'!"

Bitch, when I was tryn'a holla' at'cha' ass you what'nt on shit, Marcus contemplated to himself. "I mean, it ain't like dat, I jus' be having' shit to do," Marcus said.

Damn he smells good as hell! Donisha excitedly thought to herself as she got a whiff off Marcus's Obsession scent.

"Well, you think you can make some time out your busy schedule for me . . . ," She asked seductively while showing off her lush glossed-up lips. "Or do Peaches have that shit on lock?" she asked in a jokingly fashion.

Before Marcus could give a reply, he was interrupted by the vibrations of his pager going off. Although Marcus had been ignoring Donisha unknowingly, he couldn't deny how cute and sexy she looked. With her freshly done weave wrap, skintight jeans that caressed her perfect curves, a small red halter top that flaunted her perky breasts, which imprinted her hard nipples, and a fresh pair of red and white '93 Jordan's on her feet, she was dressed real ghetto fabulous.

"Damn, I gotta get out'a here," Marcus mumbled out while looking down, scanning through his pager. "Uhhhh . . . Yeah, yeah we can do some'nt. What'chú doin' tonight?" Marcus asked while still in a trance from the numbers in the pager, ignoring the smart comment she made concerning Peaches.

"I'mma be sittin' on my porch bored to death as usual," she stated in a sarcastic tone.

"A'ight, I'll be through there later on to get'chú."

"Damn, Donisha, that ass gettin' fatter by the day!" Marlin interrupted with humor as he and the girls marched their way toward the two.

"Boa, don't play wit' me."

"You what'nt sayin' that shit last night!"

"Yeah right, you wish you could get some of this."

"Aey, let me holla' at'chú for a minute, Jo," Marcus said, directing all his attention to Marlin.

"Damn, Marcus, hi to you too!" Jessica blurted out.

"Wassup, Jessica?"

"You jus' don't fuck wit' us no' mo, huh?" Jessica asked sarcastically as if she was getting on Marcus's case.

"It ain't like dat. You kno' I love y'all," Marcus replied humorously, making the group of females chuckle before stepping off to the side with Marlin.

"Aey, I gotta make a quick run. When Shorty gets low in work, get up wit' Lil G to re-up on the weed. I got Mikey takin' care shit in the back so don't worry 'bout that, a'ight," Marcus explained.

"I got'chú," Marlin responded. "You gon' hit that pussy tonight, ain't'chú."

"I ain't thinkin' 'bout her. I got other hoes to attend to. Besides, I'mma make her ass wait a lil while longer anyway, ya dig," Marcus said while walking in the direction of his Chevy. "I'mma get wit'chú in'a

minute, lord."

"A'ight."

Every day Marcus's block was popping like a block club party. That kept a lot of attention off the operation in the alley. When the detectives would ride through Avers, they only paid attention to the traffic that circulated on the front of the block. When the Ds found out that it was only weed being sold on the block, they stopped sweatin' so hard. Detectives cared less about weed being sold; they wanted to catch the hustlers that sold blows and crack.

After a straight month of consistent working, Avers Street started doing anywhere from five to ten thousand dollars a day off blows alone and the same off crack—not including the weed that was doing a couple of thousand a day due to the break of the weather. The weed was Marcus's least concern; I guess you can say he had the weed on the block for the sake of the 'hood.

Marcus had a successful get-money strategy that his guys couldn't refuse. He would give each one of his guys (Marlin, Mikey, Pee Wee, Lil G, JR) one day out of the first week of each month to profit all of that day's earnings. The only thing Marcus asked of his crew was to make sure he received a couple of thousand after each one of those days to put up for store money and another thousand dollars for his personal use. Those days would fall on the first thru the fifth of each month, so that usually meant double the money.

His guys would bring in roughly ten thousand after each one of those days for their own pockets. For the remainder of the month, all the money got turned in to Marcus, and every Friday he would pay his crew a two-thousand-dollar paycheck. His crew was making more money than they ever saw in their life! So it was safe to say Marcus was loved tremendously by his crew, and if they could help it, they weren't going to let any harm come in Marcus's direction.

Marcus and his crew were making this type of money for about three months straight without any major heat from the neighborhood detectives or the feds. At this point of Marcus's hustling career, his name was beginning to ring bells to all the major hustlers throughout the Westside.

Chapter 8

Sylvia seemed to be the only wise person in Marcus's life. Even though he was young and doing the wrong thing, she still wanted to give him the best advice on how to invest his money. Marcus would always listen to her suggestions, which sometimes sounded like motherly demands. He never reacted to her plans for him; he always kept them in the back of his mind. Although Marcus was young, he was smart enough to know that the money he was making weren't going to last a lifetime.

One early morning, Steve drove through Avers, hoping to catch Marcus. "Aey, make sure security stay on point." Marcus stood on the block, instructing Pee Wee on keeping the joint secured. "If the Ds are able to get close-up on whoeva's workin', that mean they ain't doin' their job. Get rid of they ass quick and don't pay'em shit if that happens."

"I'm already on it, lord," Pee Wee said as he took a pull off his Newport.

The six o'clock dope traffic started accumulating through the alley while Marcus and Pee Wee continued to converse. The dope (heroin) always brought in the most money during morning hours. Dope fiends must get their sickness off before the start of their day.

Out of nowhere a two-door white Acura Legend with dark tint speedily turned the corner in the process of pulling up directly where Marcus and Pee Wee were standing.

"Who the fuck is this pullin' up like they crazy?" Pee Wee stated in a hushed tone while gripping the handle of his pistol on his waistline.

"Whoever' it is fenna' get it," Marcus replied calmly while looking away from the car, but easing his hand toward his waist, seconds from drawing his protection.

Neither of the two recognized the car and was ready to unload at any second. After about a ten-second standoff, the driver-side window began to slowly lower down.

"Don't kill me, young blood," Steve stated with a murderous grin covering his mug. "I'm jus' tryn'a holla at'chú."

"What the fuck," Marcus whispered to himself while looking at Steve with a disgusted expression.

"Man, Unc, we ain't kno' who the hell you was, rolling' up on us this early in the morning," Pee Wee jokingly said while adjusting his pistol back in place.

Marcus continued his conversation with Pee Wee like nothing happened. Marcus really had nothing else to talk to Pee Wee about; he was basically making Steve wait. Steve waited in the car patiently for about fifteen minutes.

"Damn, you too busy to give me a minute?" Steve asked Marcus in an irritated tone.

"Let me see what this nigga want," Marcus said in a low-pitched tone, talking to Pee Wee. "I'll be right back."

Marcus shook up with Pee Wee before heading to the car.

"I wonder what the hell this nigga want," Marcus whispered to himself as he reached to open the passenger-side door of the Acura.

Steve had been making several attempts to get in contact with Marcus in the past by riding through Avers, but to no avail. He knew if he had any chance of catching up with him, it had to be during early morning hours.

"Wassup?" Marcus asked aggressively as he settled inside the car.

"Wassup wit'chú?" Steve replied

"Shit, you said you wanted to talk, so talk!"

"Man, look, I didn't come ova' here to argue wit'chú or be kissin' yo' ass. I jus' been thinkin' 'bout chú and I don't wonna see you get fucked up out here in these streets!" Steve expressed himself rigorously while looking at Marcus staring out the passenger-side window.

"You sho' it ain't the other way around?" Marcus asked while still looking the other way, avoiding eye contact with Steve.

"What!" Steve snapped. "You think I wonna see some'nt happen to you out here?" He asked without getting a response. "Your family loves the shit out of you. And yo' momma, lord knows she'll be devastated if somethin' happen to you in these streets."

"I'll be straight," Marcus simply replied without showing any emotions.

"Why you got so much animosity built up toward me . . . ?" Steve asked, showing much concern. "I been in your life since you were a little boy and you always showed resentment toward me."

"Don't act like you don't know what the fuck been going' on!" Marcus all of sudden snapped while quickly turning his attention toward Steve. "You think 'cause it's been so many years I was gon' forget?"

"What the hell you talking about?" Steve fired back with an angry and confused expression.

"My pops' murder!" Marcus countered angrily. "Now explain that since you wanna talk so bad!"

"That's what this been about all these years? You think I killed yo' ole man?"

"If you didn't do it, you know who the fuck did!"

"Look, Marcus, let me tell you something'. I know how important it is to have a father figure. I would never want you to grow up without your father . . . ," Steve began to explain. "Yo' ole man was a renegade, a real go-getta'. He never joined a nation and didn't give a fuck what a nigga claimed to be. If he wanted to get'chú bad enough, yo' ass was through! Even though we never saw eye to eye, I must say yo' ole man was a stand-up guy. I jus' hate that he started fuckin' wit' that shit 'fore he died." Steve spoke as if he was reminiscing while staring into space.

Marcus sat there in complete silence for a moment. He couldn't deny the fact that his pops started snorting blows (heroin) toward the end of his life.

Marcus and Steve conversed for a couple of hours. In the midst of their conversation, Marcus revealed how he didn't appreciate how Steve showed favoritism toward Chris when they were younger. Steve was very apologetic and really didn't have an explanation for his past actions. Steve knew how the two bosses worked, and he didn't want Marcus being blindfolded. Marcus took everything Steve was saying into consideration. Believe it or not, he accepted his apology, and they moved on. Marcus knew Steve had been involved with the Vice Lord Nation for at least twenty years, so he had the knowledge of the streets. Marcus figured Steve had to have some type of love for him because of his mother, Sylvia, so he felt like he could put some trust in Steve's future advice.

After their conversation, Marcus began living his life a little happier and moving even smarter and swifter in the streets. Everyone, including Sylvia, saw how their relationship had mended; they were spending more time with each other in the streets and with the family. This made their household much more lovable!

As time went on, things seemed smooth, but of course everyone wasn't on the same page.

Spoonie, the person who kick-started Marcus's hustling career, was beginning to whisper things to Smitty about Marcus.

"Wassup, Chief?" Spoonie greeted Smitty while taking a seat at Edna's Soul food Restaurant located on Kedzie and Madison.

"Ain't nuttin' to it. You eating' some'nt'?" Smitty asked while stuffing his face with a mouthful of smothered, baked chicken with garlic mashed potatoes and sweet corn.

"How badly I wanna stay and eat wit'chú, but I'mma have to take a pass today. I jus' came to drop off this package to you and 'spit a bug' in ya' ear," Spoonie said while sliding under the table a large plastic footlocker bag with two Nike shoe boxes full of money.

"Too busy to sit and eat huh, that must mean business is goin' good, I like that," Smitty said jokingly as he took another bite of his food. "What is it that you gotta tell me?" Smitty asked, wiping his mouth with a handkerchief, with a more businesslike approach.

"I was jus' wondering' how often do you see Marcus since he been doin' his own thang?" Spoonie asked curiously.

"I see him maybe once or twice a week," Smitty replied while taking a sip of water. "I'm tellin' you, that boy doin' his damn thang to be so young. He runs through about a brick 'n' a half and at least two to three hundred grams of dope a week! Dat's damn good for a joint that jus' opened up. Why you ask have I been seeing him, what's goin' on?" Smitty asked after praising Marcus's hustling abilities.

"Nuttin', I was jus' wondering' 'cause he ain't been coming' thru Twenty-first to holla' at none of the brotha's ova' there in a while. It seems like since he started rotating wit' them conservatives he been straying away from the nation 'slowly but sho'ly.' I jus' hope he ain't forgot who put'em on!" Spoonie said in a low but aggressive tone.

"Well, I do understand that he's been rotating with his ole man lately but I ain't got no problem wit' that. We all a family, and the loyalty still there," Smitty explained. "But you can never be too sure about nuttin' these days, so that'll be something' I'll keep on my brain."

"That's all I'm saying', Chief. I ain't tryn'a start no confusion within' the nation but this is what the streets is saying' and seeing' wit' their own eyes," Spoonie explained while noticing Smitty being in a deep thought. After a few seconds of silence, Spoonie said, "Let me get outta here. I got'a few runs to make. You need anything else befo' I ride out, Chief?"

"Nah, you don enough. I'll holla at'chú a little later," Smitty said with a serious expression on his face as if he was contemplating on his thoughts.

Some would say it was envy that was starting to boil up in Spoonie because of the success Marcus was having in such a short period of time.

Marcus wasn't aware of what was being said at the time because he felt that he was doing the right thing and everything was love. No matter how much money Marcus was making, he continued to get all his work from Smitty and attended every mandatory meeting. In Marcus's eyes, everything was going smooth, and since both nations had joined as one, he didn't feel that it was a problem if he ran with the conservatives a little more.

Chapter 9

The summer of '93 was coming to an end. Smitty wanted to see if there was any truth to what Spoonie had been whispering to him. Smitty had an assignment for Marcus and Marcus only.

"It's kind of' dead out here tonight, ain't it?" Marcus asked as he and Lil G smoked on a blunt while riding down Pulaski, a main street on the west side of Chicago.

"Hell yeah, that's 'cause it's a Sunday night, everybody partied out," Lil G replied as he took a long drag off the blunt and at the same time glancing in his rearview and side mirrors while steering.

It was a gloomy and wet Sunday night; Marcus rode the passenger side of a clean but low-key '92 four-door Maxima, which he sponsored. Lil G drove through different side blocks on the west side while they smoked and brainstormed on past and present events that had been going on.

"It's getting late anyway. I'mma 'bout to call it one in'a minute," Marcus stated while yawning and rubbing the top of his head, which was filled with waves. From Marcus's expression, you could tell the weed was taking effect and making him tired.

"Late . . . ," Lil G retorted while glancing down at his wristwatch. "Shhiiit, it's only nine-thirty, lord."

"I know, but hell it feels like it's about twelve-thirty."

"Where you lay ya' head at tonight?" Lil G asked.

"I don't know yet. I gotta make a couple calls to see which one of my hoes gon' act right, ya know!" Marcus said in a pimping fashion as they both shared a brief laugh.

As Marcus reached for his phone, it rang before he had a chance to put it to use.

"Yeah, who dis?" Marcus answered on the first ring.

"You already know who this is, wassup wit'chú, boa'?" The person on the other end stated confidently.

"Chief, what's going' on?" Marcus said with much alertness as he hand-signaled Lil G to lower the volume of the radio.

"Everything a'ight?" Marcus asked with major concern, recognizing Smitty voice instantly.

"Yeah, yeah, everything's cool. Aey listen, where you at right now?"

"We jus' passed by Independence and Madison. I'm jus' hittin' a few blocks befo' I call it a night."

"Who wit'chú?" Smitty asked

"Its jus' me and Lil G."

"Aey, I'm leaving' the south side from a lil get-together. You think you can meet me off the Independence exit in about ten minutes? I need to run somethin' by you."

"You know I'm already right here. I'm waiting' on you," Marcus replied respectfully.

"A'ight, I'll see you in'a minute," Smitty said as they hung up from each other.

Marcus got off the phone and sat in complete silence for a couple of minutes, thinking about his unusual meeting with Smitty. He figured it had to be something important for Smitty to meet up with him so late. Even though it was only about ten o'clock, Smitty always made his way home before eleven o'clock, and he never did business after nightfall.

"Lord, what got'chú ova' there so focused, something' wrong?" Lil G asked curiously.

"The hell if I know. Smitty want me to meet'em off Independence in ten minutes."

"Yeah, some'nt gotta be wrong. You know he don't usually be out this late."

"I know," Marcus agreed

Lil G turned a few extra blocks in the area to waste time. Marcus flamed up another blunt that was already rolled up; they both smoked in silence while thinking about the situation at hand.

With a thousand and one things rambling through Marcus's mind as he smoked, his train of thoughts was interrupted by his phone ringing.

"Yeah, you made it?" Marcus answered the phone anxiously, assuming that it was Smitty on the other end.

"I didn't know I was heading anywhere in particular." On the other end was the voice of a young lady by the name of Nicole, whom Marcus had recently met that Friday in traffic.

"Oh, I'm sorry. How you doing'?" Marcus greeted in a friendlier manner.

"You know who you talking to?" she asked as if it was a trick question.

"Of course!" Marcus claimed as if he was certain.

"I'll still be waiting if it was up to you to call me, huh?" Nicole said with humor.

After she made that statement, Marcus then knew exactly who he was on the phone with.

"Nah, it ain't like that, sweetie. I jus' had a lot of runnin' 'round to do this weekend and it slipped my mind," Marcus replied.

"Aw, okay. I didn't catch you at a bad time, did I?"

"Not at all. What'chú gettin' into tonight?"

"Actually I'm just leaving my aunt's house, on my way home, bored as ever'."

From the moment Marcus asked Nicole to pull over out of traffic so they could meet, he knew from their conversation that she was intelligent and had a high level of schooling under her belt. Even though Marcus never made it past the twelfth grade, he wasn't illiterate by a long shot and knew how to talk with much sense.

"I know' a beautiful woman like yourself not goin' in alone?" Marcus asked seductively.

"Unfortunately yes, and it sucks!" She answered with a slight giggle.

"Well, you know the night still young. How about we get together so we can become better acquainted with one another?" Marcus spoke on the phone with his eyes low from the weed smoke, looking as if he was in his slick-talking player mode.

Lil G was barely paying attention to the road from listening so hard to Marcus's conversation, wondering who he was slick-talking on the other end of the phone. Marcus's crew knew he had the "gift of gab" for getting fine women that stayed outside the 'hood. They were always anxious to see how the females looked because nine times out of ten they had nice-looking friends somewhere for them.

"I don't mind. What you tryn'a do?" Nicole asked, sounding sexy as ever.

Nicole was fine as hell. She stood about five foot nine with a dark brown complexion, long jet-black hair that dropped down to her lower back, a beautiful smile with deep dimples, and perfect white teeth. About a size C-cup breasts and a nice plump ass with thick thighs and no stomach. A real stallion, she put you in mind of a Gabrielle Union.

Before Marcus could give a response, he was interrupted by a beep from the other line.

"Sweetie, hold on for a second, okay?"

"Sure."

Marcus had to gather himself before answering the other line so he could focus on the matter at hand.

"Yeah," Marcus answered.

"Yeah, where ya at, boa'?" Smitty spoke.

"We coming around the block now, 'bout to pull up on the side street off the expressway."

"A'ight, I'm waiting on you. I'm sitting in my black car."

"Okay."

Marcus ended the call and directed Lil G to Smitty '93 four-door black-on-black Jaguar, as they turned on Congress, the street alongside of the I-290 expressway. Lil G parked two cars behind Smitty.

The moment Marcus proceeded to enter the jag; he instantly smelled the fresh scent of new car leather with a mixture of Joop fragrance. *Damn, this nigga stay fresh*, Marcus thought to himself after witnessing Smitty dressed in a stonewashed blue jean Guess suit with matching light blue alligator cowboy boots. With his one-carat stud in his left ear and a low cut with a full sharply lined beard, Smitty looked and smelled like a million bucks.

"Wassup, Chief? What's da bin'nis?" Marcus said, settling in on the passenger side of the Jag.

"You Wassup . . . !" Smitty replied by smiling and extending his hand toward Marcus to perform the IVL nation handshake. "I see ya lookin' good, which means you doin' some'nt right," Smitty said jokingly as they both shared a brief laugh.

"I'm jus' followin' suit, tryn'a do the right thing, ya kno'."

"Yeah, I hear dat . . . ," Smitty said while smoothly rubbing on his neatly cut goatee. "Aey check it out right, I gotta little dilemma that I need took care of."

"Whatever' it is, consider it done," Marcus said with confidence.

"'Thats why I luv you," Smitty replied, shaking up with Marcus for the second time. "We blessed you wit' three-star elite status and you still showing the same loyalty that you had from the start. I can't say that for everybody. Some brotha's get blessed wit' some juice and start going' against the grain. Ya kno', they seem to forget who put'em on. So therefore, them the guys that end up getting' spanked," Smitty explained, staring Marcus straight in the face with his horror eyes that would intimidate the toughest gangster around.

"I already know," Marcus uttered out, matching Smitty stare but with much honor and respect in his young eyes.

"But anyway," Smitty said, snapping out of a trance. "I need a job done. This type of hit takes a little homework, though. Any other time I would jus' send a hit squad through and tear a nigga whole area up, but he ain't worth starting a war over so I don't want it to be so obvious."

Marcus sat there mind-boggled and wondering why he was singled out to do the nations dirty work. Marcus had enough power and vicious killers on his team to send out his own hits. Marcus never minded getting his hands dirty, and actually he was pretty good at it, but something about this mission didn't intrigue him.

"Jus' let me know' when you need it done, Chief."

"I'll get up wit'chú in'a couple days so we can rotate a little bit and scope some things out," Smitty insisted.

"Dat's wassup."

After shaking up with Smitty, Marcus exited the car with mixed feelings. He couldn't turn away from the mission—that would've showed signs of disloyalty. "What the fuck is this shit about anyway?" Marcus asked himself while approaching the Maxima where Lil G awaited.

"...I promise I'm coming' through there tonight . . . ," Lil G spoke on the phone. "You jus' be ready when I get there."

After meeting with Smitty, Marcus had no intensions on getting up with his new prospect, Nicole; all he could dwell on was the meeting with Smitty.

"Aey, I'mma call you back when I'm on my way, a'ight." Lil G ended his phone call after noticing Marcus being in deep thought.

Fuck it, ain't nuttin' to think about. Time to get in kill mode, Marcus thought to himself.

"What's goin' on? Everything a'ight?" Lil G asked with a serious, concerned expression on his face.

Marcus didn't say a word, but the look he gave Lil G let it be known what time it was. Lil G didn't say another word about the situation as he drove; he knew what it was, and he stayed ready for whatever.

"Lord, drop me off at the apartment. I need to get me some sleep," Marcus said while sparking up another rolled-up blunt. "Come pick me up early in the morning so we can get the block in order."

"You ain't gon' get up wit' that broad from earlier?" Lil G asked as if he was reminding Marcus of a good situation

"Nah, I got some shit on my mind that I need to map out," Marcus replied, exhaling a cloud of weed smoke. Marcus had his own low-key apartment in Forest Park, a small suburb on the outskirt of the west side of Chicago. Few people knew about his high-rise apartment located off Lake Street and Circle Avenue. Marcus rarely stayed there alone; he always had company with him—rather it was just him and a young lady or him and the crew with a bunch of ladies. This particular night was different.

Chapter 10

In the meanwhile, Marcus kept everything to himself; for some reason, the mission he was being sent on just didn't feel right. Marcus was an elite now, so he never had to be hands on with certain situations anymore. Marcus had people in his crew to do all his dirty work.

Lately it was not normal for Steve not to be in contact with Marcus for more than a few days. Steve would drive through Avers hoping to bump into Marcus; he would ask the workers and whoever was running the block out of the crew about Marcus's whereabouts, and the answers he would always get was either "you just missed him" or "he's been gone since earlier." The end result was that Marcus was rotating with Smitty all of those days.

Smitty always did his homework on important figures before he made them victims. Any other situation he would just send word to have guys dealt with.

"Yeah, this where his baby momma stay at," Smitty mentioned while driving down Kostner Avenue, then making a right turn on Fifth. "Push come to shove this where we might have to catch'em at."

Marcus rode on the passenger side while Smitty drove through K-Town, lurking in a low-key short-body red '91 Cadillac Seville with dark tint. Most of the ride, Marcus sat in silence smoking on a blunt and being very observant of his surroundings. Smitty drove by every possible spot that J-Roc could go.

"Look, there the nigga go right there," Smitty said while driving down Gladys Street, a side block off Kostner. "This one of the blocks that he hustles on . . . muthafucka over there laughing' and joking'. Don't even know' what's in store for his fat ass," Smitty stated in a murderous tone.

Marcus, still sitting in silence, looked over to study his victim's demeanor. From what Marcus could see J-Roc seemed like the type of leader that needed attention to feel important. J-Roc was a heavyset guy that stood about six feet tall. J-Roc was a solid three-hundred-pound dude that moved swiftly. He ran his crew of guys with force and intimidation. After Smitty circled the block a few times, they even witnessed J-Rock beat the shit out of one of his workers for coming up short with his money. J-Rock was one of the New Breeds main enforcers, and Smitty knew if he got him out the way, it would slightly weaken their army. Smitty was the sneaky type; he never let people know he had a problem with them. He just intruded when necessary.

On the way driving back toward Avers, Marcus never asked any questions about the matter. At that point, it didn't make a difference what was the cause of this mission; it had to be done, and he was the chosen one to do it. After about a week of riding and lurking with Smitty, Marcus found out all of J-Rock's locations and hideouts, that's all he needed; now it was time to execute.

Pulling up on Avers, Marcus noticed the white Acura Legend that Steve had been rolling around in lately, parked on the block.

"A'ight, Chief, I'll make sho' I let you know' when I'mma 'bout to make a move," Marcus said while exiting the vehicle.

"Yeah, you jus' make sho' you keep ya' head up out here and stay focused like you been doing'," Smitty responded, looking around at all the different types of traffic Marcus had circulating through Avers Street.

Before Marcus could get out of the car good, different people, from hypes to little children, was on the block calling his name, trying to get his attention. By Marcus mind being elsewhere, he inadvertently avoided the commotion that was headed his direction and instantly made his way to where Steve was stationed.

"Whudd up, ole man?" Marcus said once entering the passenger side of the car.

"I been tryn'a get up wit'chú. You had me out here worried 'bout chú, everything straight?" Steve asked, looking concerned.

Marcus hesitated about telling Steve about the mission that he was being sent on, but it was eating him up, so he had to let it out.

"Yeah, everything cool, I guess," Marcus said, still hesitant. "I was rotating wit' Smitty the last few days."

"I know who you been wit', that's why I'm asking' is everything cool."

"Smitty want me to ride down on this Breed nigga from out of K-Town."

"You, personally ?" Steve asked while looking puzzled. "Or he jus' want your crew to handle it?"

"He wants me to whack this nigga," Marcus assured. "For what . . . the hell if I know," Marcus explained, showing signs of confusion.

"What's the nigga name?" Steve asked

"J-Rock. He be ova' there off Kostner and Gladys."

"I heard of that name befo' . . . ," Steve said while recollecting. "Is he a big dude wit' braids, real dark skinned and always keep a mean mug on his face?"

"Yeah, that's him!"

"I wonder why he tryn'a start a war wit' them guys?" Steve asked himself as he contemplated.

"That's why he claims he wants me to do it because he didn't wanna start a war."

"So what he think, them guys ain't gon' try to find out who the fuck did that shit!" Steve snapped. "And I think Big C got some type of connections wit' them Breeds ova' that way. You know what, hold off a minute befo' you make a move; let me check on some things."

Marcus agreed to delay the hit as long as he could, but in all actuality, he had his mind made up to take care of that business. Marcus looked at the situation like a personal favor to Smitty, and if he got the job done, it would not only display his loyalty to Smitty but to the nation as well.

A week went by, and Marcus didn't want to waste any more time. He was trying to wait on Steve's information, but he could feel the pressure in the air, so he had to make a move.

While riding with Smitty, Marcus found out that J-Rock goes to a nightclub on Friday nights called the Dragon Room on the north side of the city. J-Rock also had a low-key apartment close by the club that too many people didn't know about. These were usually his weekend trick-off spots.

On a Friday night in late September, Marcus stood on Avers, laughing and joking with his crew like he normally does on Fridays. "Where them hoes at for the night, Pee Wee?" Marcus asked as he stood in the midst of his crew while they all enjoyed the fruits of their labor by smoking good and drinking on a gallon of Hennessy.

"Pee Wee ain't got no hoes. That nigga be fuckin' wit' all dem fat bitches 'n' shit," Marlin blurted out, causing the crowd to burst into laughter.

Marcus knew from his comment that he would cause a humorous commotion within the crowd. Pee Wee was the least person out the crew that went to clubs looking for women, and Marlin was always the one to let it be known. Mikey and Lil G was more of the club hoppers that had females lined up for late-night action.

Pee Wee and Marlin continued to crack on each other, trying their hardest to get the others to side with every point they made on each other. As they continued on, Marcus kept glancing at his watch, keeping track of the time.

"I jus' felt some raindrops, it look like it's about to do some raining out here," Marcus said, breaking up the back-and-forth joking.

"Yeah, it's supposed to rain the rest of the night," Mikey responded amongst the other conversations that were going on in their circle.

Hell yeah! This perfect weather for me to gone do what I gotta do! Marcus thought excitedly to himself.

"Marlin, you running the block for the night shift, right?" Marcus said.

"And you know iiiitt! This little rain ain't stoppin' shit, I'm out here!" Marlin answered, showing signs that he was a little tipsy from the gallon of Hennessy the four of them were sipping on.

"A'ight, make sho' you check wit' Lil G when you get to the last few packs. I'm 'bout to make a move real quick. Lil G, let me get the keys to the Maxima and you drive the Crown Vic tonight," Marcus demanded.

Marcus had three different work cars on the block for his crew to rotate in. Marcus jumped in the Maxima and left out the neighborhood.

About an hour after Marcus left off Avers, Big C and Steve turned the corner in hopes of catching up with Marcus to let him know the mission was bogus. The person Marcus was sent off to kill just happened to be a distant relative of Big C. Smitty was aware of the relationship Big C had with J-Rock; that's why the situation seemed so suspicious.

See, Marcus had the mind-set and the patience for this type of work. Marcus sat on the block where J-Rock hustled on; the rain started coming down hard, and as planned, J-Rock drove up around 11:30 p.m. Pulling up in a clean two-door midnight blue '83 Monte Carlo sitting on nineteen-inch hundred-spoke rims, banging a Chicago-style mixtape by JD Wax master (a popular Chicago land area DJ), J-Rock hopped out the car while leaving it running as he entered one particular house on Gladys Street.

J-Rock stayed in the house for all of ten minutes before racing out to the car due to the rain, to approach his Monte Carlo. Before J-Rock could pull off, two Chevys filled with guys, everybody in both cars moving to the rhythm of their loud sound systems with all their hats cocked to the right, pulled up next to the double-parked Monte Carlo.

"Wassup, G!" The driver hollered out from the first Chevy that pulled up. "Where we headed for the night?"

"Jus' follow me," J-Rock replied as he skated off, slightly burning from his tires.

J-Rock and his crew had no clue that they were being scoped out by a parked car on the same block where they hustled.

Instead of being aware of their surroundings, their minds were set on drinking more liquor and partying with some hoes.

Marcus kept a good distance behind all three cars as they weaved wildly on the wet pavement between other cars while driving down Kostner, headed toward the 290 East Expressway. Marcus followed the cars without them having any suspicion. As they continued to drive wildly, Marcus noticed each car switching lanes entering Interstate 90, heading toward the north side. As they exited the North Avenue exit ramp, Marcus followed them all the way to their location, which just happened to be the Dragon Room nightclub. The club was located on North Avenue, a main street off the expressway, which meant no parking on the main streets, only in the club's parking lot.

Marcus paid for parking as if he was attending the club; instead he reclined his seat all the way back and watched the large crowd gathering.

As time went by, Marcus waited in the car patiently while smoking and sipping on his cup of Hennessy. Out of nowhere his pager began going off rapidly. "Who the fuck is this paging me like they crazy," Marcus said as he ignored the unfamiliar number. Little did Marcus know, the unfamiliar number was Steve trying to inform him to hold off on the mission, not knowing Marcus was already in position for the kill.

Nightclubs in the city usually shut down around three o'clock on Friday nights. The time was approaching; it was a quarter 'til three, and the club was starting to let out. People began staggering outside, and it was obvious by their actions that majority of the people had a few drinks too many.

A crowd of loud and drunken guys stood in front of the club, trying to converse with every fine female that crossed their path. In the middle of the group of guys stood J-Rock, the person whom Marcus had his eyes on throughout all the commotion that was in progress.

After about fifteen minutes of standing outside the club, mingling, J-Rock and his clique connected with a group of the tipsy females that they were conversing with. Once making it to the parking lot, they continued to laugh and joke with one another.

"Aey, G, let me holla at'chú real quick," J-Rock whispered to one of his guys as they walked off from the crowd in the direction of his Monte Carlo. "Here go the keys to the apartment, I'mma about to ride out."

"You tellin' me you ain't fenna get up wit' them bad-azz hoes wit' us!" one of his guys said with excitement while glancing back at the crowd.

"Nah, not tonight. I got my bitch waitin' up at the crib for me. She been trippin' lately."

"A'ight, G, I guess I'll holla at'chú tomorrow, then."

"Now, call my phone tonight and let me know y'all made it to the crib safely," J-Rock insisted as they performed the New Breed handshake before going their separate ways.

J-Rock jumped into his Monte Carlo and skeeted out the parking lot, burning rubber, with his music blasting. As he was leaving, so was Marcus. On the way out the parking lot, Marcus noticed J-Rock left alone—that made the situation seem even sweeter in Marcus's eyes.

Something unusual was happening; instead of J-Rock going in the direction of his low-key apartment, located ten minutes from the club, he jumped on the 290 West Expressway, heading toward the west side of the city.

The expressway was clear, and it seemed as if these were the only two cars on the expressway. The visibility was impaired because of the major fog due to the rain. The thick fog made it difficult to see the cars ahead of you.

J-Rock ended up exiting off at the Cicero exit ramp. Marcus knew from the exit that either he was going to the block where he hustled or his baby mom's crib, which was only a couple of minutes off the expressway. J-Rock made a right turn onto Cicero and then a quick left on the cross street, Arlington. Nine times out of ten, J-Rock was headed to his baby mother's house.

Marcus raced over to the block where the house was located to scope everything out. The house had an enclosed front porch; Marcus saw that the lights were on as if someone was waiting up.

Marcus parked his car a block away and changed into his proper attire—an all-black hood and a black ski mask. Marcus then stuffed his snub-nosed chrome .38 revolver on his waistline, got out the car, and crept through a gangway to an alley that connected with the back of the house. Marcus then posted up on the side of the house; where he was kneeling down at, he was able to see all angles of the street without being noticed.

J-Rock passed by twice before parking directly in front of the house. *"Damn, I should've got up wit' them hoes. Fuck it let me go in here 'fore I won't have to hear her gaddamn mouth,"* J-Rock mumbled to himself as he contemplated on his present situation. When Marcus saw J-Rock was getting out the car to approach his destination, he pulled the ski mask over his mug and pulled his pistol from his waistline. As soon as J-Rock took one step on the porch, Marcus ran out the gangway immediately! J-Roc saw Marcus as he got close-up on him. "Ohhhhh Shit!!!" J-Roc shockingly yelled out as he froze up in likes of someone seeing a ghost.

Marcus let off three close-ranged shots; all three of the shots landed in the chest area. After the third shot, Marcus heard the footsteps of a person running to the door right before hearing a woman's voice screaming at the top of her lungs.

As the woman frantically made it to the door, she witnessed a man in all black with his face covered with a ski mask, standing over J-Rock with a gun to his face while J-Rock held his chest grasping for air with his eyes growing to the size of golf balls. "Noooooooo!!! Please, GOD, No!!!" The hysterical woman shouted out with her hands placed over her face in the midst of witnessing the execution. Without any hesitation, Marcus released the fourth shot to J-Roc's facial, which put him out of his misery. Immediately after the last shot, Marcus then fled the foggy scene into the wet and dark alleyway, only to hear the desperate sound of a woman screaming, "Please, somebody help meeeee!!! Please!!!" These were the screams of J-Rock's baby mother.

Chapter 11

It was the fall of '94, and another school year was beginning for Christopher. He wasn't too eager about starting another school year, but he was very anxious for the basketball season to get underway. Chris was in the eighth grade now, and you could say he was the most popular kid attending St. Angela. Chris and Bridget were still involved with each other, even though she graduated and went on to an all-girl high school.

"Chris, I know you see Alexis ova' there staring at'chú, right?" Antwone asked while he, Randy, and Chris walked the halls in St. Angela, on their way to recess. Randy and Antwone were classmates as well as teammates of Chris. "Alicia told me Alexis been saying' y'all go together."

"I don't know why she saying' that. I ain't fuckin' wit' that girl!" Chris responded while walking down the hallway trying his hardest to avoid eye contact with Alexis.

Alexis was as skinny as a toothpick, dark skinned, and never kept her hair done. She was the type of girl that had a flipped mouth, always talked back to all the teachers, and kept rumors floating in the air about other students.

"Aey lord, niggaz all around my crib be talking' 'bout'cho' brotha 'n' shit, saying' how he's gettin' money now and how slick his Chevy is," Randy mentioned as they made their way to the outside parking lot to enjoy a pickup game of tag football at recess on a sunny, mid-seventy-degree fall Monday afternoon. It was the time of season where all the leaves turned brown and orange and started shedding to the ground.

"Who you heard say dat shit?" Chris asked curiously.

"Dem Mafias ova' there on Central and North Avenue."

"Yeah we gettin' money," Chris claimed as he threw a long pass to one of his classmates. "Dem hatin'-ass niggaz betta' keep my brotha' name out they mouth 'fore we come ova' there and fuck they ass up."

"Man, them lame-ass niggaz don't want no trouble. Dey know how crazy those Insanes off Twenty-first is!" Randy laughed out as he spoke.

"Heeeeyyyy, Chris!" a young girl out the seventh grade walked up, interrupting their conversation to speak to Chris.

"Whudd up," Chris responded with a strange look on his face.

"Here, this for you," The young girl said as she handed Chris a folded-up sheet of paper. "That's from your secret admirer," She said as she laughed and turned away.

"What the fuck!" Chris exclaimed with a frown as he opened to read the letter.

"'I can't wait 'til the day I can taste your sexy body with your fine ass!" Chris read the letter out loud with Antwone and Randy standing beside him. They both burst out laughing while Chris stood there looking puzzled.

"Man, this shit ain't funny. Who you think wrote this shit?" Chris asked his buddies standing next to him.

"Nigga don't act like you don't know," Antwone joked as they continued to giggle.

"Don't play wit' me, Jo," Chris said with a grin as he balled the note up. "That hoe knows better'."

Through Chris's actions, you could tell the street life was starting to fascinate his imagination. Every day in school he would boast and brag on how his brother was getting a lot of money and always mentioning all the nice cars he had. Chris even began claiming that he was affiliated with the IVL nation; a few of his seventh—and eighth-grade friends followed. Marcus wouldn't have agreed with Chris's actions if he'd known; all he wanted Chris to do was to complete high school and possibly go on to college—not only to pursue his hoop dreams but also to accomplish getting a degree in business administration. Marcus had big dreams for his younger brother, and he definitely didn't want to lose him to the street life.

In the meanwhile, Sylvia was enjoying life by getting out in the world more and doing things that made her content and happy. Marcus would drop off ten thousand dollars a month to his mother for her to put up in case of any emergencies. Even though Sylvia knew where her son's money was coming from, she still accepted it. Marcus allowed Sylvia to spend money on whatever her heart desired. Instead of Sylvia spending money on unnecessary things, she invested majority of his money into different savings accounts that drew interest quarterly. Sylvia never informed Marcus of her doings. Marcus wasn't too concerned on how his mother handled his money because he had plenty of money put up in five other spots, not including all the money he had circulating through the streets.

A couple of months had passed since Marcus drove down on J-Rock. The word in the streets was that the New Breeds blamed the Black Souls (another street mob) for the murder of J-Rock. A couple of weeks prior to J-Rock getting shot to death, him and his crew got into an altercation with the Souls over a neutral block located in K-Town. J-Roc had even sent some of his soldiers to shoot at the souls on their own set and ended up killing a few of their people. When Marcus was informed by Smitty about the situation, he began moving around in the streets normally.

The couple weeks Marcus lay low after completing the mission for Smitty, business was still being handled by his crew, but not as smoothly. Three pack workers had gotten popped off (locked up) on Avers while posted in the alley hustling. Usually, when the ole-school addicts worked, they never held the work directly on them; but since Marcus hadn't been around for about a month, everybody started slightly slipping. All three workers had long criminal backgrounds of drug offenses, so they were held at the Cook County Jail without bond, but one in particular was released for no apparent reason.

"Yeah, I jus' made it on'a block, 'bout to get shit situated," Mikey spoke on the phone as he exited the Chevy, one of the crew's work cars, to supply the block for the day shift. "I'mma call you back in'a minute." Mikey ended the call as he proceeded to approach a particular house on Avers.

It was a typical fall Chicago day, about fifty-five degrees, cloudy, wind blowing fiercely, grass filled with different colored leaves. Days started getting shorter; something in the autumn weather always made the atmosphere feel gloomy.

As Mikey made his way out the house onto the front porch, he saw Dirty Red from afar. Dirty Red was one of the three pack workers that got popped off while working blow jabs in the alley of Avers.

"*How the hell he get out so quick?*" Mikey asked himself while looking across the street at Dirty Red standing next to a couple of his neighborhood friends. As Mikey began to step down the steps on his way to drop off two g-bundles to one of the Shorty lords that distribute the packs to the workers, Dirty Red hollered from across the street, "Mikey lord!" attempting to get Mikey's attention. Mikey initially ignored him as he assertively got into the Aluminum. "Lord, let me holla' at'chu!" Dirty Red quickly marched his way excitedly to the car before Mikey could pull off.

"Wassup, man!" Mikey retorted irritably while shifting the car into drive. "You kno' I'm dirty, I gotta go drop this shit off!"

"Lord, I'm ready to get back to work."

"You ready to get back to work?" Mikey arguably asked with a disgusted expression. "How the fuck you get out so quick, anyway?"

"You know I'm too slick for them mothafuckas to find some shit on me! I was down to my last two rocks and I swallowed them bitches. Mitch and Hotrod had jus' started on fresh packs, that's how they got caught wit' all that shit." Dirty anxiously said while fidgeting with his nose and constantly rubbing his face. By his actions it was obvious that he was in desperate need for a fix.

"Yeah, I hear you, man, but let me get outta here so I can do what I gotta do," Mikey responded, not giving any thought to what was just said.

"Lord, you know I'm jus' getting' out. I'm sick den'a muthafucka, let me get a blow and I'll work the next pack for nothing'," Dirty Red pleaded.

"I ain't got no free blows and I damn sho' don't need you to work!" Mikey exclaimed aggressively, easing his way out the parking space while Dirty was still rested on the driver's side window seal.

"You think dem niggaz a take this seven dolla's we got?" Dirty begged desperately. Mikey simply shrugged his shoulders and sped off.

Dirty Red stood in the middle of the street looking confused and sick. He had to find a way to not only get high but to also get back into the pack-working rotation.

One Friday morning, everything seemed normal. A typical day for Marcus was waking up every morning before sunrise to meet up with one of his crew members (usually JR or Lil G) at a location to give him all of the day's work. The clientele on the block had built up over time, so at this point, Marcus was sending out twelve thousand worth of blows (heroin) and twelve thousand dollars worth of crack a day. Exactly ten thousand dollars from each drug, after the runners and pack workers pay, would come back to the table for Marcus. Majority of the time the money wouldn't be short a dollar because everyone was getting paid well.

On this particular morning, Marcus met Lil G at a premier breakfast spot called Epples, located on the southeast side of Chicago, five minutes from downtown, ten minutes from the 'hood. Epples was the go-to spot after a night of clubbin' for big-timers; also a lot of business people conducted early morning business over the smells of fresh coffee and the aroma of delicious breakfasts being prepared.

"hey, sweethearts," the older waitress greeted Marcus and Lil G as they seated themselves at a booth close to the window where they were able to see the main street.

"How you doing this morning, Ms. Gloria?" Marcus said, knowing the waitress's name by hard. Most of the time he would demand to be seated at whatever section she served.

"Y'all need a minute, honey, or y'all just getting the usual?" Gloria spoke as she placed the menus in front of them both and poured coffee.

"The usual for me," Marcus replied by handing her back the menu. The usual for Marcus meant two turkey sausage patties, three eggs scrambled lightly with cheese, three hotcakes with sliced cinnamon apples on top, potato hash browns with grilled onions cooked inside, and a large glass of freshly squeezed orange juice.

"Mrs. Gloria, let me jus' get a steak 'n' cheese omelet wit' grilled onions cooked in my hash browns and a large apple juice wit' no ice."

"Everything in the omelet?"

"Everything except green peppers."

"Pancakes or waffles?"

"Pancakes.

"All righty, shuga', let me take these menus and put you all orders in. It shouldn't take that long before y'all food be ready," the waitress said as she walked toward the kitchen area with the menus and coffee kettle in hand. By the sounds of the orders being hollered in the kitchen to the cooks, the clanking of the pots and pans, the different conversations, and papers being shuffled, that was the normal busy atmosphere at Epples.

"Man, lord, I had a long night yesterday, boa!" Marcus said with a smirk as he sipped on his coffee.

"awe shit, whatchú don' got into now, hot boy?" Lil G responded excitedly while rubbing his hands together in anticipation to what Marcus was about to tell him.

"Man, Jo, I'm on my way to crib in Forest Park to change clothes, right,"

"Right, right," Lil G muttered out while preparing to give Marcus his undivided attention.

"Instead of jumpin' on the e-way (expressway), I took Madison all the way to the suburbs. I was at the red light on Austin and I jus' happen to glance out the passenger-side window and saw this fine ass red bone staring at me . . . ," Marcus explained while performing different hand gestures to get his point across. "So I wave, she waved back; I instantly raised the window down and told her to pull ova'. To make a long story short, the bitch got out the car thick and fine as hell!" Marcus explained with excitement. "I asked her name and where she was headed. She tells me she was on the way to pick up her girl and they were looking for somewhere to relax and have some drinks!"

"What!" Lil G retorted with a surprised expression.

"So I mentioned that I had my own spot and I told her they were more than welcome to join me. She looked surprised at first, and then she asked me did I have somebody for her friend. Of course I said yeah. I ended up exchanging numbers wit' the broad and told her to call me when they was ready. Soon as I lef' her, I tried callin' yo' muthafuckin' ass and you ain't even answer the phone!"

"'Round what time you called the phone?"

"Nigga, I called yo' ass from nine thirty 'til the time I got up wit' dem hoes," Marcus claimed. "Then I started callin' Mikey phone and that nigga didn't wanna answer either. I shoal hate if it was an emergency. I would've jus' been fucked up, huh?!" Marcus said with a slight seriousness in his tone.

"Naaahhh, lord, it ain't like dat. I was ova' there fuckin' 'round wit' them niggaz on Twenty-first, out there drinking' and smoking 'n' shit and forgot my damn phone in the car . . . ," Lil G explained. "But yo, dat nigga Spoonie was out there talkin' real slick at the mouth last night."

"Yeah?" Marcus reacted in disbelief.

"All right, fellas," the waitress said while placing orders on the table, interrupting their conversation temporarily. "Can I get you guys anything else?"

"Everything looks good right now, thank you," Marcus said.

"All righty, gimme a holla if y'all need me."

"Now what'chu was sayin' about Spoonie?" Marcus stated while preparing his food with salt 'n' pepper.

"He was jus' sayin' shit like, how you ain't been fuckin' wit'em since we been doin' our own thang and how you forgot who put'chu on . . . ," Lil G explained while digging his knife and fork into his omelet. "Ion know how everybody else took what he was sayin' but I sensed a little jealousy comin' from him."

"I wonder why he ain't say none of that shit when he seen me ova' 'there hollin' at Peaches the other day."

"You kno' how these niggaz be. But fuck all dat. What happened wit' them hoes, nigga," Lil G said.

"Awe yeah, them hoes came through. We smoked and took shots of tequila all night. Dem hoes got hot and started doing each other . . . !" Marcus spoke with excitement. "When I seen that, I knew it was on! I ended up fuckin' both of dem bitches 'til it was time for me to get up wit'chú."

Lil G sat there stunned with his mouth wide open momentarily. While the night of Marcus's orgy was still on Lil G's mind, Marcus had other thoughts on his brains as they continued to eat. He felt that it was time to start keeping a close eye on his own brothers in the nation.

After they were done eating breakfast, Marcus gave Lil G the supplies he needed to take to Mikey.

Everything went according to plan—Mikey met up with Lil G and got what he needed. Mikey was en route to do his normal routine—go separate the work and drop it off to the pack runner. As he exited the car with a large shopping bag in hand, walking toward one of the stash houses two blocks over from Avers, two Chevy Caprice with no license plates came speeding from opposite directions filled with detectives, jumping out, pointing guns. "Get down! Get down!" the two lead detectives ordered as Mikey slowly kneeled down and put his hands behind his head. At that instant, Mikey knew there was little he could do, so he cooperated. Of course when the detectives searched Mikey and searched the car thoroughly, they found what they were looking for—drugs and a pistol.

"Uhh huh . . . !" Packman said as he discovered the hidden packs inside the bag full of groceries. Packman and KT were the most notorious detectives on the west side of Chicago at that time. They were known for extorting big-time drug dealers for money and planting drugs and pistols on young hustlers they wanted out the way. "Look what we got here!" Packman hollered out to his partner KT, who was busy searching the car.

Packman ordered one of the other detectives to put Mikey in handcuffs and made him lie facedown in the grass while he walked over to KT with the packs in his hands. After searching the

Chevy Aluminum thoroughly, KT ended up finding a chrome .40 caliber that was kept

under the driver's side seat at all times.

"Pick his sorry ass up . . . !" KT said to one of the detectives.

"Step over here with us so we can holla at cha," Packman said as he and KT grabbed Mikey by the arms and walked him off from the other standing detectives. "You know with this pistol and the rest of that shit we found; your black ass ain't gon' see these streets for a mighty long time," Packman said with a smirk on his face while spinning the pistol on one finger.

Mikey gave the two detectives a stale expression while keeping silent while the Ds continued to harass him.

"Look, we know what the fuck is going on! You ain't the muthafucka we want . . . ," Packman said while intensely looking at Mikey's face. "All you gotta do is tell us who our man is and you can get the fuck on, wit' no strings attached."

"Man, look, I ain't got shit for y'all so go 'head and do what you gon' do," Mikey said with a slight arrogance in his tone.

"Awe, okay, you wanna be a smart ass huh . . . !" KT angrily said as they both pushed Mikey around. "Let's lock his ass up!"

Mikey kept silent the entire way. The detectives ended up taking him to the station to book him on a narcotic charge, but the pistol magically disappeared!

Chapter 12

Marcus always expected some type of heat from the detectives sooner or later; but from two stash houses getting raided, the pack workers getting caught up, and Mikey's arrest, it seemed as if the police were getting some type of inside information. Marcus weren't quite sure what was going on, but he was going to put his finger on it and get to the bottom of the situation.

Mikey had been sitting in Cook County Jail for the past three weeks without bond. Mikey was still on probation from a previous dope charge he caught a couple of years back, so he was being held without bond. Mikey had done time before at the county jail, so he knew the proper procedures to go through once he made it to population.

In Cook County Jail, there's certain individuals who's in charge of the gang operations in each division. Every time Mikey went to the county, he was the one over whatever deck he was on; he would get a high slot that everyone there respected. Of course the reason behind that was because they knew about his reputation from the streets; everyone knew about his reputation from the streets. By him being a part of the IVL nation and his involvement with Marcus's personal crew, which made everyone know that he was not to be fucked with.

Whenever someone came on the deck that holds rank, they were informed on everything that's going on behind the walls; every time, that's being said about important figures in the inside and on the outside world. Sometimes guys in jail knew more about the shit in the streets before it even went down.

"Count time! Count time! Everybody go to their assigned cells until count is over!" the two correctional officers insisted as they started their roll calls.

In Cook County, the COs knew the type of shit that went down; most of them were crooked officers, so they were either getting paid for their services or they just didn't give a fuck.

"All right, good count, fellas . . . ," the COs said as they were leaving out of division eleven's D block. "Get ready for yard call!"

"Aey, lord, remember dat nigga I was tellin' you 'bout . . . ," Mikey's cell mate said.

"Yeah, what about him?"

"Every time I see dat nigga, he claims that he gotta holla' at'chu 'bout something. He say it got somethin' to do wit' what's goin' on ova' there on Avers," his cell mate explained.

The first time Mikey was informed about somebody trying to get up with him, he ignored it, thinking that it wasn't important. When he found out that it had something to do with the block that he hustled on, it made him eager to see what was going on.

"Come on, let's go to the yard so you can show me who this dude is."

As the two inmates strolled through the dorm on their way to yard call, they were constantly stopped by other vice lord brothers, whom they shook up with and had small conversations with.

The yard scene was always sectioned off with different groups. You had guys playing full-court basketball, lifting weights, and different gangs would call meetings amongst their mob to make sure everybody was on point for when it was time for the deck to get sent up (gang war). The moment Mikey and his cell mate stepped foot on the yard, at least twenty Insanes, conservatives, and other vice lord brothers gathered up around

Mikey to discuss different issues. In the midst of all the different conversations that were going on in their circle, an older guy walked up to join the crowd.

"Hotrod, wassup, man?" Mikey said, recognizing the older guy immediately. Hotrod was one of the three pack workers that caught a charge while working over on Avers. They greeted each other by shaking up.

"Man, I been tryn'a get up with'chu ever since I heard about what happened," Hotrod claimed as they proceeded to walk off from the crowd. Mikey got a light to his roll-up cigarette as they continued to talk.

"Yeah, they jus' moved me from division nine a couple weeks ago . . . ," Mikey said while exhaling a puff of nicotine smoke. "I know these muthafuckas gon' have me sittin' in this bitch for a minute 'cause of this probation shit, but it's cool. I know soons I get a bond I'm getting' the fuck on. You know if y'all had a bond we would've been came and got y'all niggaz."

"You know that goes without being said, my nigga . . . ," Hotrod said as they shook up once again. "I heard it's been getting' heated out there since that shit happened to us."

"Yeah, them people been sweatin' the block hard lately. But'chu know that shit was bound to start happenin' sooner or later."

"I been meaning to ask you have you heard from that nigga Dirty Red since he been out?" Hotrod asked curiously.

"Hell yeah . . . !" Mikey said while handing Hotrod the short to his cigarette. "That ma'fucka came ova' to the block talking' 'bout he ready to get back to work. At first I was like, hell naw, but after he kept sweatin' me to let him work, I ended up letting' him get back out there."

Hotrod shook his head in disbelief while taking the last few pulls off the short (cigarette) before throwing it to the ground. From his reaction, you could tell something was wrong.

"Look, man, the police was tryn'a get all us to talk." Hotrod stopped them both in their tracks while he explained. "I thought all of us was gon' stay solid, until the police came and got

Dirty Red out of population in the middle of the night and took'em to PC. Next thing I know he was being released."

"Some'nt told me that nigga turned sour," Mikey stressed to himself while listening to Hotrod carry on about Dirty being a snitch. Mikey knew it was some truth to what Hotrod was telling him because of how the detectives tried to get him to rat.

Their conversation was interrupted due to the police rushing everybody back to their dorms because of a brawl on the yard that involved a group of Latinos. Mikey shook up with Hotrod for the last time after handing him a few roll-ups and letting him know to send over a kite if he needed anything else.

Mikey then walked back to the dorm and immediately got on the phone to send word through one of his females from the 'hood who knew how to get in touch with Marcus. Through limited conversation and talking in codes, Mikey was able to get his point across clearly.

It was the spring of '95, two months before Chris's graduation from the eighth grade. Chris was barely passing his classes. He'd do just enough to stay eligible for the basketball season. Chris weren't interested in doing schoolwork at all, but he was having his best basketball season thus far.

When Chris would be at home, if he wasn't in the backyard playing basketball with his neighborhood friends, he would stand in front of the house, hoping to catch Marcus pass through the block so he could beg to ride around with him. Every time he attempted to ask in the past, Marcus would blow him off with excuses. The reason behind him making excuses was that he never wanted anything to pop off while Chris was with him. Marcus stayed strapped, so he never worried about shit happening to him when rotating by himself or with his guys.

After an hour of Chris sitting on his front porch, fooling around with some girls from off the block and a few of his buddies, just as he planned, Marcus came flying toward their block in his newest toy—a four-door black and gray 500 1995 Benz with twenty-inch Loren Hart rims with the loud sounds of MJG and Eightball' hit record, "Lay It Down," blasting through his four twelve-inch subwoofers.

That car was the latest model that Mercedes-Benz came out with at the time, and Marcus was the only young black person in the city with one at the early age of twenty-one. The Benz was a big change from his last attraction, which was a '93 mint green drop-top Mustang 5.0 with eighteen-inch gold Dayton's and neon lights underneath the car that came on at night. Every car Marcus ever had that was expensive had the loudest sound system in the 'hood, if not the entire city.

Chris and his friends stood up off the porch, staring and nodding their heads at the sounds of MJG & Eightballs, "*Lay it down! Lay it down! You hoes lay it down . . . !*" When the car got close enough for Chris to notice that it was his brother driving the Benz, he immediately raced to the curb to flag Marcus down. Marcus slowed up in front of his mother's house with one arm rested on the window seal and one hand on the steering wheel, nodding his head up and down to the sounds of his music.

"Wassup, lil bro!" Marcus said while adjusting the volume to a lower level with a remote control that came with the Alpine face-off.

"Man, when you get this ma'fucka!" Chris yelled out with an astounded expression on his face as he checked the Benz out from front to back.

"I jus' picked it up not too long ago. I had been ordered it a couple months ago. You prob'le the first person that seen me in it."

"And I'mma be the first to ride with'chu too."

"Nah, nah, you know I got moves to make."

"Come-on, man, jus' hit a few blocks wit' me. I'm bored as hell," Chris sympathized his way in the car, not taking no for an answer.

"Damn! You jus' gon' leave yo homies standing' there?" Marcus asked, looking over at Chris with a smirk.

"They'll be a'ight . . . ," Chris responded as he waved his hand, referring to his friends. "Aey, y'all, I'll be back!" Chris yelled from the passenger seat. His group of friends was so busy analyzing the car that they didn't respond back. Marcus then eased off, replaying "Lay It Down" from the beginning, turning it all the way up. *"We doin' dis shit once again fa you fake-azz niggaz, lay da fuck down bitch . . . !"*

As they drove through a few blocks in the neighborhood, Marcus could see the excitement that ignited Chris as he rapped along to his favorite rap song, noticing all the attention Marcus was getting. Everybody that knew Marcus, and those that didn't know him, threw up the deuce sign in acknowledgement while staring at the Benz drive by like it was a spaceship that fell out the sky. Marcus even drove through Twenty-first Strip and saw Spoonie standing outside on Homan. Marcus blew the horn and threw up the deuce to Spoonie, only to get an unpleasant nod in return with an expression of disbelief on his face.

Marcus knew if Steve not only see his new Benz but also see Chris rotating blocks in the 'hood with him, he wouldn't have heard the last of his mouth. It wasn't that Steve didn't want Chris hanging with Marcus. It was for safety purposes. In the '90s on the streets of Chicago, if you were joyriding through different 'hoods in a nice car and you wasn't a made man, anything was bound to happen. Marcus knew he had to travel outside their neighborhood into a neutral area to be in a safer zone.

As they continued to ride the city, Chris could tell they were headed in the direction of their Grandmother Emma's house on the near west side of the city.

Chapter 13

"Baby! See who's ringing the doorbell, I'm in the shower .
. . !" Smitty hollered from out of his state-of-the-art bathroom that
connected to his master bedroom. Everything in the bathroom,
from the floor to the countertops, were all marble, and all the
fixings and faucets were all made with twenty-four-carat pure gold.
Smitty had an extravagant home!—five bedrooms, two-car garage,
with a built-in indoor swimming pool in the backyard. His home
was located in Orland Park in the far southwest suburbs. The
commute from where he stayed to the west side of Chicago was at
least a couple of hours. Nobody in the nation knew about this
Capone Suite—only his immediate family. A selected few knew
about Smitty ten other key cribs throughout the city. Marcus was
one of those few.

"I wonder who the hell coming to my house this late in the
afternoon . . . ," Smitty asked himself out loud while still in the
shower. "Prob'le some kids going' door-to-door tryn'a sell some
shit . . . ," Smitty continued to think out loud. "Sweetie! Who was
at the door?" Smitty yelled; he thought nothing when he didn't get
a response back from his lady.

Three minutes after not getting a response, Smitty woman
was being escorted to the master's bathroom by five armed,
unidentified older white men.

"We have a warrant in the name of 'Alphonso Smith' a.k.a. Smitty!" one officer chanted aggressively while they all showed badges and pointed their guns toward Smitty.

"What the fuck is this! Y'all gotta be terribly making a mistake!" Smitty frantically said with a strange look on his face as he got out the shower, reaching for a dry towel.

The unidentified officers were dressed in suits and ties; some were wearing blue jeans and collar shirts with jackets that had U.S. Marshals written on the back. It was clear that these were officers with the FBI and the U.S. Marshals.

"You're being indicted on conspiracy charges of being linked to the Portelli family drug cartel operations out of Columbia and also charges on being the ringleader of the notorious Chicago street gang called the Insane Vice Lords!" the head officer spoke proudly as if he knew they had concrete charges.

The FBI officers recited to Smitty and his lady their rights while they allowed him to put on some clothes.

"Why y'all handcuffing her! She ain't got nuttin' to do wit' this shit!" Smitty claimed as they proceeded to handcuff him.

"Believe me, the snapshots we have, she's right along in them with you. I'm sure she knows what's going on!"

"I need to get my lawyer on the phone, right now!" Smitty demanded as the officers proceeded to escort them out the house.

"You'll be able to take care of that once we make it downtown," one of the FBI officers said, while walking side by side with Smitty and his girl, directing them to an unmarked Dodge Intrepid.

"I don't think your high-profile lawyer would even be able to get your ass out of this jam, Mr. Smith! We've been building this case on you and your foreign connect friends for the past ten years. You guys finally slipped up and gave us a lead. Everything else we had was too weak to put you all away for the time you're looking at now. Watch your head getting in the car!" the lead FBI detective said all of this while smiling the entire time.

Marcus and Chris ended up riding down Independence Boulevard, then eventually making a turn unto the cross street Madison Avenue. Madison is a popular street on the west side of the city that runs from downtown Chicago through to the 'hood where all the Arabic-owned shopping centers are located, and it ends in the west suburbs. The United Center, where the Bulls play ball, is also located on Madison Street.

Marcus made a quick stop at Tops and Bottoms, a popular clothing store that most young hustlers go to, to get their fresh gear. Marcus was dropping by to pick up a wardrobe he had prepared. Of course when Chris saw that he was going in with Marcus instead of waiting in the car, he knew it was on!

"Habeeb, wassup, man?" Marcus greeted the Arab owner as they entered the store.

"Marcus, my homey! What it is?" Habeeb said in a heavy Arabic accent, trying to talk with street slang.

"Yeah, whatever, I know you betta' have my order in and don't be tryn'a charge me them high-ass prices, either!" Marcus said with a slight humor as he walked to the back of the store where all the expensive gear was.

"Don't worry, buddy, don't I always take good care of you, brotha'," Habeeb claimed.

While Marcus was checking his order as Habeeb was bringing it to the counter, he noticed Chris admiring some of the expensive clothing that he normally wouldn't be able to get from their mother.

"Aey, Habeeb, have one of yo' workers to help my lil brotha' out wit' whatever' he want," Marcus said to where only Habeeb could hear him.

"No problem, Jo. Did I say that right?" Habeeb joked with Marcus as they both shared a laugh. He then instructed one of his workers, in their language, to take care of Chris.

Chris reacted like a small kid at a candy store, grabbing damn near everything that was in his eyesight. His total alone came out to be five hundred dollars. After everything was said and done, Marcus ended up dropping forty-five hundred on clothes within thirty minutes. This was a light shopping day for Marcus that wasn't planned. He was spontaneous like that at times; he just did whatever he felt.

Marcus wasn't headed anywhere in particular, so they continued driving down Madison Avenue, where traffic stayed flowing, day in and day out!

"So, what's goin' on wit' school?" Marcus asked Chris while setting the radio on mute, catching Chris by surprise as he was in the middle of rapping along to one of his favorite songs. Chris never thought Marcus was too concerned about his school grades.

"Awe, everything straight. You know we undefeated this season. I be killin'nem fools on the court, they have to call for a double-team jus' to try to stop me! The play-offs starts in'a couple weeks, I know you gon' be there, right?" Chris said all of this, hoping to throw Marcus off from asking about his grades.

"Yeah, all that sounds good, but I was really asking about them grades."

"Well . . . ," Chris hesitated, "I ain't gon' lie to you, the first semester I was getting all Ds, but I'm picking them up now. By the end of the year I should be a'ight."

"Look, Chris, man, Momma worked too hard for you to be fuckin' up in school . . . Shit, its bad enuff I was a disappointment to her.

"I guess what I'm tryn'a say is, give a better' effort in making' Momma happy. I know I haven't been a good example for you but at the time, I did what I felt I had to do. I'mma change eventually but right now, I'm in too deep . . . I have to make the best out of the situation I'm in now. You have a choice, lil bro, and it starts right now!" Marcus spoke with emphasis as if he was giving a mini-lecture. Everything he said was heartfelt, and Chris gave him his undivided attention. This was their first real-life conversation since Marcus started getting a lot of money.

While Marcus was busy talking, he ended up taking Madison all the way down to Central Boulevard. As Marcus turned on to Central, he noticed someone who looked like an old buddy of his in the car driving next to him.

"Damn, Chris! Don't that look like my buddy Shawn driving in that BMW next to us?" Marcus asked while looking and pointing toward the passenger-side window.

"Shawn?" Chris responded confusedly.

"Yeah, Shawn from off Division, around Granma house." Marcus instantly raised his passenger-side window down while blowing his horn, trying to get his buddy's attention.

After doing a double take, the person driving next to them noticed who it was blowing the horn trying to get his attention.

"Ohhhh shit! Wass up, boa'!" Shawn yelled out the window with excitement.

"Whudd up, my nigga . . . !" Marcus hollered back, matching Shawn's energy. "Pull over at the next street!"

"A'ight!"

Marcus switched lanes to get behind Shawn when he noticed the BMW Shawn was driving was a 1995 740iL model. Marcus figured Shawn had to be getting some type of money to be riding in a BMW. It wasn't on the level as the 500 Benz Marcus was in, but it wasn't too far off. They both pulled over at the next main street, which was Washington Boulevard.

"Gaaaddamn! Life must be treating' you good, homey!" Shawn said as they greeted each other with a handshake followed by a formal hug.

"Shhhiiit, I should be saying' the same about you. What this is, next year's shit?" Marcus replied, referring to Shawn's BMW. They both were in respectable luxury cars. Marcus knew his Benz was much gaudier and expensive.

"Man, where yo' ass been hiding' at? Every time I ride through Division I stop and ask yo' people have they seen you. Everybody claim they don't be seeing' you like that," Shawn claimed

"Yeah, man, I'm still ova' there in the Holy City."

"I see you doing' yo' muthafuckin' thang too . . . !" Shawn expressed with excitement as he rubbed the side of his face. "Gaaaddamn, how can I be down, my nigga!" Shawn joked as they both shared a brief laugh.

"From the looks of it, you're already down!" Marcus said while checking out the BMW from front to back.

"Yeah, I do a'ight for myself . . . ," Shawn said while keeping his eyes on the ongoing traffic. "Aey, where you on your way to?"

"I got Chris in the car wit' me, 'bout to ride through Division and stop to holla at my people."

"Chris, wassup, boa . . . !" Shawn said, throwing up the deuce. "Dat lil nigga still look like he bad as hell!"

"Hell yeah!" Marcus eagerly agreed.

"Aey, I'mma follow y'all ova' that way. We need to catch up on some things."

"A'ight," Marcus said as they gave each other five before getting back inside their cars.

As they maneuvered through the traffic, Marcus was telling Chris how tight he and Shawn were back in the day. Shawn was a magnet for the girls and loved to play basketball. He stood about six foot three, medium built; light brown skinned, and had deep-set eyes. The surrounding of his eyes was a darker shade, in looks of someone that don't get hardly enough sleep. Shawn's mother was full-blooded Cherokee Indian, and his father was black. So Shawn had a good grade of short wavy hair.

As they pulled up on the 1100 block of Monitor, a side block off of the main street, Division, Chris immediately went inside their grandmother's house after seeing that the block was empty and none of his old friends were out. Marcus and Shawn stood in front of the house and resumed their conversation. It was a mild seventy-degree spring afternoon with the sun fading in and out the clouds. They both were geared up in spring like gear: Marcus dressed in some Girbaud jeans with a blue and white Air Max Nike T-shirt that matched his '95 blue and white air max's with the air bubble around the entire tennis shoe; Shawn on the other hand had on a white and black new-era White Sox baseball cap with the authentic white sox baseball jersey to match and some all-white leather '95 Air Max. By the way they were dressed, it was obvious that they weren't out to impress but they were still fresher than the average dude.

Every time Marcus drove through Division and stood out in front of his grandmother's house, he attracted a crowd. This particular day was no exception. Some of the people out there had love for Marcus, and some of them hated him, but the ones that hated laughed and joked to keep from showing it. A lot of people felt like Marcus had turned his back on the 'hood once his mother moved him to the other side of town, in the Holy City. Marcus had found new friends around where he moved, so he rarely went back around Division to hang out. Marcus showed his face more once he started getting a lot of money hustling. A lot of guys thought he was riding through just to shine on them. Shawn didn't have many known haters in the Division area, and mainly because he was affiliated with the Four Corner Hustlas, another mob that ruled majority of the Division area and other scattered parts of the city. Shawn's uncle Ray had rank amongst the Foes and had his own separate land that he controlled. Shawn left from around Division at an early age and had been doing business with his uncle ever since.

Majority of the land on Division was controlled by a set of identical twins by the name of Dre and Drew, short for Andre and Andrew. They were in their early twenties, and they both were short and as black as charcoal. They always kept an arrogant type of expression upon their faces that let everyone who crossed their path know they were 'hood rich. The only way to tell the two apart was from the way they walked; Dre had gotten shot up really bad a while back during a gang war, and with one of the bullets still stuck in his leg, he was forced to walk with a terrible limp. The twins had high rank with the Foes, and they were getting major money on their blocks. One of the main reasons for their success was that they were the only few people in the city still selling their product in capsules. Every capsule that was sold, they made sure the customers got three times more than what they paid for. This assured them all the clientele in the area.

After thirty minutes of standing, at least twenty guys and 'hood girls, had accumulated as a crowd around Marcus and Shawn. Everybody was smoking weed, and some had cups in their hands prior to walking up. Everybody was joking and having a good time reminiscing on past times, until Grandma Emma came outdoors to join the party.

"Marcus, I know damn well you ain't been out here all this time without coming in here to talk to me . . . !" Grandma Emma yelled out humorously from the front door, standing in her famous long black nightgown. "And all y'all know better than to be all bunched up in front of my house like that. Y'all know I don't play that shit!" She directed her statement to the normal faces that she saw on a daily basis.

"We sorry, Mrs. Williams . . . ," a few from the scattering crowd blurted out while trying to hide their cups and the blunts.

"I told'em, Granma. They didn't wanna listen to me," Marcus said jokingly as he walked up, attempting to hug and kiss his grandmother.

"Don't gimme that . . . !" she teased as she reluctantly turned her cheek, trying to avoid his kiss. "Yo' ass out here right along wit'em . . . !" she stated with humor. "And who big, nice cars parked in front of my house?"

"I . . . I don't know. One of theirs I guess . . . ," Marcus hesitated to say. "I parked my car down the street." Marcus wanted to avoid any questions his grandmother had about him being able to afford a hundred-thousand-dollar car at the age of twenty-one. "Granma, you remember Shawn, don't you?" he quickly asked, trying to redirect her attention away from the cars.

"I thought he looked familiar. How you doing, sweetheart?"

"I'm all right, Granny," Shawn replied respectfully, trying to hide his highness. "How you been feeling?"

"Awe, I'm hanging in there, shuga. A few aches and pains here and there, but I'm handling it . . . All right, let me get back in here and finish talking to this other knucklehead grandson of mine. I just came out here to mess wit' y'all for a minute," she stated while making her way back inside the house.

"A'ight, Granma, I'll be in there in'a minute," Marcus assured her while directing his attention back to conversing with Shawn.

Marcus and his grandmother had a special, open type of relationship with each other. He felt like he could go to his granny and talk just about anything because he knew she would keep it real with him at all cost.

Shawn began to talk to Marcus about a plan he had in mind to open up shop on a block around Division. Shawn claimed he had his own crew of hungry young Foe's that he was going to bring over that way to grind for him. He mentioned that he wouldn't mind having an enforcer like Marcus to go into business with him. Shawn explained to Marcus how he earned good money working under his uncle Ray, but now he felt it was time for him to branch off and become his own boss around new scenery that he was pretty familiar with. Shawn also mentioned how he didn't want to do business with the twins.

Marcus listened to what was being said and responded by telling Shawn that he was an elite now with the IVLs, so he had access to work on any block in the Holy City. Marcus felt like Division wasn't capable of making the type of money that he was used to making on his land, especially with the twins having shit on lock. Marcus let it be known that they would either have to out do the competition or get them, out the way! Shawn knew Marcus meant business, so if Marcus was going to be included in his plans, it would be a chance of a huge problem in the future with Marcus and the Foe's. Even though Shawn was part of the Four Corner Hustlaz mob, if it was to go down, there was no question that he would ride with Marcus against the twins.

In the midst of their conversation, Marcus was interrupted by a phone call.

"Yeah, who 'dis?" Marcus answered his phone, slightly agitated after not recognizing the number.

"Yeah, where ya at, man?" the voice on the other end asked aggressively.

"I'm around. Who the hell is this?" Marcus asked irritably.

"This Steve, I need to get wit'chu, it's an emergency!"

"I'm headin' from off Division, gimme ten to fifteen minutes."

"Meet me in front of the school on Sixteenth and Millard. We'll be out there waiting' on you."

By the pressure that consumed Marcus's face and his frantic gestures, Shawn sensed that there was something wrong. Marcus was mind-boggled after the phone call. He didn't know if Steve had gotten word about his new Benz or found out Chris had been rotating with him or if something had really went down. Either way it went, Marcus was nervously eager to see what was going on.

"Everything a'ight?" Shawn asked with a look of concern covering his face.

"I don't know, my people say it's an emergency . . . ," Marcus said while racing toward his grandmother's door. "Aey let me get'cho' number so I could get up wit'chu."

After exchanging numbers with Shawn, Marcus went into the house to get Chris, and they chirped out.

Marcus took the quickest route to the 290 east Expressway, which was straight down Central. Marcus being silent and the way he was speeding and weaving crazily through traffic all the way to the Independence Exit gave Chris a funny feeling that something had went down.

After dropping Chris off, Marcus parked the Benz on Avers and jumped into his low-key Maxima to go meet up with Steve. As soon as Marcus turned down Millard Street, he saw Steve standing beside Spoonie, Big C, and three other high officials that were under Big C.

"*Damn, this can't be good*," Marcus said to himself as he parked the car and proceeded toward the crowd. Marcus walked up and greeted each one individually with the nation's handshake.

"Marcus! The talk of the Westside, Wassup, boa?" Big C greeted with suspicion in his ways.

"The talk of the Westside?" Marcus muttered out with a puzzled face.

"You know you can't ride around in'a new 500 hunit Benz without the city runnin' back telling' me . . . ," Big C said with a certain happy sort of anxiousness. "So, wheres at?"

"I parked it on Avers," Marcus answered as he glanced at the others' facial expressions that were standing in their circle. Spoonie was the only face that showed signs of jealousy.

"Well, I'm always happy for one of my own when they're doing' well for themselves, especially if they're going' by it the right way," Big C said. "But unfortunately, we didn't call you ova' here for that."

"What's goin on?"

"The feds grabbed Smitty and five of his foreign-connect friends at their homes earlier this afternoon on conspiracy charges . . .," Big C continued to explain. "From what I hear, the feds had been building a case for the past five to ten years. They also indicted him on conspiracy of being the head operator of a street mob. I'm sure they're not finish handing out indictments, so I'm advising everybody to lie low until I talk to Smitty and see what the fuck is going on."

During their conversation, Big C mentioned that he was leaving town for a couple of months until things got calm.

Everyone went their separate ways except Steve and Marcus. *Damn, this some fucked-up shit,* Marcus thought to himself as he and Steve walked toward his Maxima. Marcus knew Smitty was going to be out the picture for the time being, and Big C was leaving town, so he wondered who he would start getting his work from. Marcus had no intentions to stop hustling, but he knew he had to get as far out the area to do so.

"So, what you think this shit is all about?" Marcus asked Steve, thinking as if it's been some type of inside information told to get Smitty jammed up.

"Ain't no tellin'. You jus' stay out the limelight until we find out what the fuck is going' on . . . ," Steve explained. "Your name been ringing lately around the 'hood from how well you been doing' and that Benz you jus' got really did it. I know sometimes we like to treat ourselves to nice things but I advise you to make that car disappear before you draw unnecessary heat to you and everybody else. I'mma lay low and spend more time with Chris and Sylvia, at least until Big C come back."

Marcus continued to drive in silence. He listened to what Steve was saying, but at the same time, Marcus was orchestrating a plan inside of his head for him and his crew to continue making money.

Chapter 14

It was May of '95, and the school year was a month from being over for Chris. He led his team to the championship game, unlike last year when they were knocked out in the semifinals. Marcus made Chris a promise that he would give him some cash and take him and the family out to eat if he brought home the trophy. Of course Chris set his mind for vengeance and was feeling like he couldn't be stopped. Since the talk he and Marcus had in the car, it seemed as if he began to focus more on his schoolwork. Chris picked his grades up from below average to average and was eligible to play in the play-offs.

The game fell on a Saturday evening, seven o'clock, prime time! St. Angela was facing a team that they haven't seen all year, who were undefeated as well, a Catholic school by the name of Our Lady of Sorrows, which brought up some great players in the past years. Sorrows even had Isaiah Thomas Nephew as their star player. It didn't matter to Chris who he was up against; he refused to be denied.

The game got underway, and the gym was packed to capacity! The tournament was held at Purcell Hall, an open gym located on Washington and Keeler.

Chris started the game out slow with his team having a slight lead at the end of the first quarter.

"Chris, I need you to get more involved with the offense . . . ," St. Angela's coach intensely demanded during a quarter break. "I need my power forward to set some picks for Chris to have more options. Number thirty-two is killing us off the baseline. I need my big man to slide over and help without getting into foul trouble. A'ight, we came too far to start playing timid! I need you guys to be more aggressive! On three!"

"One, two, three, defense!" the huddle shouted as they reported back to the court.

The star player for Our Lady of Sorrows was on fire to start out and looked as if he couldn't be stopped. He had twenty of his team's forty-two points at the half, while Chris struggled with only nine points, all coming from three-point field goals, with his team down by six points.

Marcus met up with Chris while St. Angela exited the locker room after halftime.

"Damn, Jo! I thought you were ready to play?"

"I am!" Chris responded irritably.

"I can't tell, you out there playin' sof' as hell! You need to go out there and show them guy's whatchú' made of. It's a lot of high school scouts out there checking you and that other dude out. And right now, he's the one shining. You need to tighten up and go out there and play wit' some heart!" Marcus scolded his little brother, not trying to spare his feelings at all.

Marcus's pep talk had to help Chris out because he came out in the third quarter on fire, matching his first half's point total in one quarter alone. By the end of the third, St. Angela evened the score at sixty apiece. The fourth quarter was all St. Angela. The passion Chris began to play with in the second half rubbed off on his teammates, and they went up by ten points and never looked back! St. Angela ended up winning the championship game by double digits. Chris received the MVP honors with amazing stats for an eighth grader!—thirty-two points, ten assists, and five steals.

Marcus called his own meeting with his crew members and soldiers on Avers Street. Marcus stood in the middle of about twenty of his key enforcers and spoke: "As y'all should know by now, chief got jammed up on conspiracy charges and he prob'le be gone for a minute. I was told to let my team know to lie low until we got word from Smitty to do otherwise " . . ." Marcus continued to speak, "Now I know everybody still gotta eat so I'mma keep the weed out here and a few other things, but nuttin' major." Marcus realized that majority of his personal crew needed his guidance to make anything happen in the streets. Marcus wasn't worried about himself because he had money put up in several different places, but he had his own personal mob that consisted of about thirty to forty lords that he had to feed. Marcus was the type of hustler that never just thought about himself when it came down to making money, and that's what made his crew that much more loyal to him.

"Aey, lord, let me holla' at'chú . . . ," Lil G said as he and Marcus walked off from the crowd. "What we gon' do 'bout our little problem Mikey informed us on." Marcus knew he had to get Dirty Red out the way for snitching. Dirty was a neighborhood dope fiend, so he felt it wouldn't be difficult to have him dealt with.

"I definitely ain't forgotten about him. I got some'nt for his ass . . . ," Marcus explained. "Meet wit' me in the morning'." Lil G didn't know what Marcus had planned, but he knew it would be effective.

Every morning before Dirty Red began working on a pack, he had to snort a blow to get him going. Marcus mixed up his normal bomb to put out on the block. He had a special package for Dirty Red though. Instead of giving him a blow to wake him up, he would give him a blow to put him to sleep for good. Marcus bagged up all the work and separated a bag of rat poison for Dirty.

Marcus met with Lil G in the morning to give him the work for the morning shift. Marcus explained the game plan to Lil G so they could execute. As planned, Dirty Red was dope sick and needed his normal morning fix.

"Aey, Dirty!" Lil G yelled from his car window as he pulled up on Avers. Dirty wasted no time running up to the car because he knew what time it was.

"Wassup, baby . . . !" Dirty said in a slick but excited tone while attempting to shake up with Lil G. "I was hoping you pulled up soon, I need some'nt bad! You know once I get goin', I make shit happen around this muthafucka."

"Yeah, I hear you . . . ," Lil G responded, not really listening to what Dirty Red had to say. "We jus' shook up a batch of this new shit we jus' got'a hold to. I need you to check this shit out befo' I put it on the block."

"Aw, hell yeah! I know this shit fenna' be good. Give it to me so I can get started. I already got ma'fuckas comin' to me tryn'a shop."

Dirty took the blow and anxiously jogged his way toward the back of an abandoned building on Avers to get high. Lil G waited before putting the work on the block to see what was going to be the reaction.

After a few hours passed by, the word around the 'hood was that Dirty Red was found passed out inside of a vacant apartment. Everybody in the area was saying that he overdosed on a bag of heroin that was too potent, but when Lil G and Marcus heard the news, they knew their plan had worked accordingly.

After the incident with Dirty, all the hypes flooded the block to buy what they thought was good dope that killed Dirty. They figured the dope was so good that Dirty Red couldn't handle it. This made the block even hotter, and Marcus had to shut Avers down for good. Marcus started his quest to search for another area to hustle in. He had the green light to work anywhere in the Holy City, but he was instructed by the two bosses not to make a move nowhere on that side of town.

A few weeks went by, and Marcus was contemplating on his next move. Shawn had been trying to get in touch with Marcus, but he never made time to get with him.

"Let me call and see wassup wit' this nigga," Marcus thought out loud while joyriding around the city, checking his phone for missed calls.

"Wassup man . . . !" Shawn answered his cell, already knowing who was on the other end. "Gaddamn, you the hardest nigga in the world to get in touch wit'."

"Man, it ain't like dat. Its jus' been a lot of shit goin' on. Wassup wit'chu?" Marcus asked.

"Shiiiit, tryn'a bump heads wit'chú . . . ," Shawn explained. "When you get time, I wanna run some'nt by you."

"I got time now, wassup?" Marcus assured

"You name the place and I'll be there."

"I'm jus' bendin' a few blocks right now, tryn'a find me something' to eat . . . ," Marcus said. "If you want to, you can meet me up at Edna's. I all of sudden gotta taste for some beef short ribs."

"How long it's gon' take you to get there?" Shawn asked.

"I'll be there in'a 'bout thirty minutes. I jus' need to make a quick stop before I get there."

"A'ight, I'll holla at'chú in'a minute," Shawn replied as they both ended their conversation.

As Marcus continued to ride around, he couldn't help but to think about what plan Shawn had come up with. He didn't mind working around the Division area, but by him doing that, it could possibly start a war between him and the Four Corner Hustlas. Marcus was loved by many people over that way, but there were still a selected few that didn't care too much for him. Going to war was the least of Marcus's worries. He just wondered what decision Shawn would make in a critical situation.

Not too long after Marcus pulled up in Edna's parking lot, Shawn arrived in his 740i BMW.

"Wassup, boa' . . . !" Shawn said as they both exited their cars to greet each other. "I was looking for you to be in that Benz; I almost didn't recognize you in this Maxima."

"Man, I had to get rid of that ma'fucka. By me being the only young nigga in the city wit'a 500 Benz, it drew too much of the wrong attention. I'mma talk to you more about it," Marcus said as they walked toward the entrance of Edna's.

After placing their orders, they continued on with their conversation. Marcus went on to tell Shawn about Smitty getting locked up and how hot the detectives had been around the Holy City area. Shawn hated to hear the bad news, but he knew by Marcus being in this predicament that he would be more open to his plan.

"Aey, remember what I told you I wanna do around Division?" Shawn asked.

"Yeah, what about it?"

"Well, I been talking to my uncle and he wit' it. He even hooked me up wit' his guys who own that twelve-unit co-way building on the corner of Menard and Division," Shawn explained.

"You talking 'bout the building with the cabstand on the main floor?"

"Hell yeah . . . !" Shawn said with excitement. "You know ever since we was younger, running in there playing wit' them arcade games 'n' shit, we ain't see nuttin' but hypes runnin' in and out that ma'fucka."

"Yeah . . . You right about that."

"Ain't shit changed, matter of fact, its gotten worse. Every apartment in that muthafucka is rented out by addicts or bitches that are on welfare."

At that point, Shawn had Marcus's undivided attention. The waitress even brought their orders to the table without them noticing. Marcus knew Shawn's conversation was heading in the right direction, and he couldn't deny getting a piece of the action.

"The building got four vacant apartments that he's gon' let me occupy. I say we work the shit out this building and get rich!" Shawn said excitedly as he watched Marcus nod his head in agreement. Marcus showed no anxious reaction to the plan because he knew that it was easier said than done.

"You hollered at the twins?" Marcus asked while taking a bite full of beef short ribs.

"Yeah, I ran into Dre the other day and let him know what I'm about to do . . . ," Shawn continued to explain. "Really, it ain't too much they can say. We're all Foes, I'mma be just a block from where they're working at anyway."

"You let him know that you was fuckin' wit' me?"

"Nawl, I didn't tell him all that, but it shouldn't be a problem. It ain't like you some new dude that don't nobody know. We all grew up together before going our separate ways."

"Yeah, but'chu know them guys never liked me, even though they never would say it," Marcus claimed as he continued to eat away.

"Them niggaz never had the heart to come at'chú like that. Now that they know you got some juice for them IVLs, they really ain't gon' want no trouble. Even if they do, they can get dealt wit' jus' like anybody else!" Shawn said with emphasis.

Marcus listened to everything that was being said, but there were still questions that he needed answered.

"I mean, I'm wit' it, but you know I still gotta handle shit that's goin' on back my way. I'm still waiting to see how this shit wit' Smitty unfold."

"While you on hold, we could be puttin' shit into play back that way. I got the connect on the dope and the cocaine. All we need to decide is whether we wanna get fronted wit' the work or buy our own shit."

"So I take it I'm going to be introduced to your connect?"

"Yeah . . . !" Shawn answered as if Marcus should have known the answer to his question. "Unless you wanna get the work through your people."

"Man, shit is dry on my end; At least 'til Big C come back in town . . . ," Marcus went on to explain. "We could fuck wit'cho' people as long as they keep good dope and low prices."

"Those two things we never had'a problem wit'—"

"Another thing," Marcus cut him off before stating, "I gotta bring some of the lords from out the Holy City to work, at least until shit get straight in the 'hood. My guys some real hustlaz and they damn sho' ain't scared to bust there guns when it's time."

"I was hoping you said that, we need some young go-getters' that's about they bin'nis. We ain't got no time for games."

"You already know . . . ," Marcus replied. "Jus' give me some time then we can open up."

"That's wassup," Shawn agreed as they gave each other five. They continued to eat while talking about other issues other than their game plan. What was understood didn't need to be talked about any longer until the time came for them to get down to business.

Chapter 15

Mikey had been sitting in the county for nearly a whole year. He was released after the two detectives, KT and Packman, were indicted on extorting drug dealers. Nearly a dozen of street guys that these two recently had arrested were discharged on technicalities. Mikey got out knowing exactly what to expect out of the streets. As soon as Marcus got word on Mikey's release date, he planned out an entire weekend of shopping, partying, and informing Mikey on his plans on getting paid outside of being on Avers.

Marcus drove with a couple of his guys, Lil G and Marlin, while on his way to pick Mikey up from off Twenty-sixth and California, where the county jail was located.

"Y'all don't see that nigga out here nowhere, do y'all?" Marcus asked as he slowly drove down California in his newly bought '95 Chevy Suburban, looking for Mikey to be outside of the county.

"Hell naw. I hope we ain't overlooking him by it being so many ma'fuckas out here. He don't know what kind of car we in?" Lil G asked, half breathing, as he hit the blunt that they had in rotation.

"That ain't him ova' there wit' all that hair on his face, is it?" Marlin asked as he stared out the backseat window.

"Hell yeah . . . !" Lil G said as he rushed to let his window down. "Aey, homey, you need a ride!" Lil G hollered out the window as they slowly pulled up in front of the barb wired gates of Division 11.

Once Mikey noticed who they were, he frantically ran toward the truck as if he had just escaped from the jail. He instantly acknowledged Lil G, who happened to be his blood cousin, by shaking up with him and giving him a casual hug.

"Fuck all that lovey-dovey shit; let's get the fuck away from all these police. We got shit to do!" Marcus said in a jokingly manner, but in all actuality, he was glad to see his man free from that cage.

"Lord! What's goin' on?" Mikey greeted joyfully as he entered the car.

"Same ole shit . . . ," said Marcus as he passed Mikey a fresh rolled-up blunt for him to blaze up. "You know what time it is, my nigga?"

Mikey didn't have to wonder what was next on their agenda; he knew by him sticking by the code of the streets and not snitching that he would get blessed by his crew, especially knowing that Marcus was the type of leader that took good care of his guys.

"Aey, lord, you know I can't wait to drive that new Benz I been hearing a lot about," Mikey said while exhaling the weed smoke.

"How you hear about it? I didn't have it for more than a couple weeks."

"Everybody that came in there from the 'hood was talking about that muthafucka!" Mikey chuckled out while passing Marcus the blunt.

"That's why I had to get rid of it. I drew too much attention."

"I like this ma'fucka right here . . . !" Mikey claimed as he glanced around inside the truck. "I see you got some bang back there. Let me hear dat shit!"

"I got'chu," Marcus responded by turning up the sounds to his four fifteen-inch kickers, and all you heard was the lyrics to 2Pac's record, "So Many Tears": "*...I lost so many kids and shed so*

112

many tears… Lord knows I tried being a witness to homicide, drive-bys takin lives, little kids died " . . *."* Everybody chanted the words to Pac's song while en route to their destination.

The remainder of that day consisted of good smoking, drinking, and fucking with some females Marcus had on standby for all five of his crew members: Marlin, Mikey, JR, Pee Wee, and Lil G. Marcus informed his guys of his plans to open up a block around Division area, and of course they were down for the cause. They were all only familiar with hustling on blocks in the Holy City; they were always down with taking over a new area.

The partying was far from over for Mikey. He insisted on going out to the club the following day. Marcus wasn't the clubbin' type at all, but for his guys, he figured that it was all right to ball out for one night.

It was a nice mid-sixty-degree night in Chicago. The wind slightly blowing, a real Chicago summer-night type of feel, everything in the atmosphere felt right. Marcus and his crew were dressed to impress this particular night. Everyone was dressed in their own style, but Marcus stood out for the most part. With an all-beige linen short outfit, all-tan Bally sneakers, deep black Versace shades, an original Rolex on his left wrist, and topped off with a one-carat diamond glistening from his left ear, Marcus had all the right accessories to top off his gear—fresh to death!

Marcus and his crew drove five cars deep to a popular club downtown called Strictly Business. Mikey rode the passenger side of Marcus in the suburban, with JR and Pee Wee in the backseat. Everybody was strapped with protection, including the cars that followed behind Marcus.

"You know this ain't my type of scene right here," Marcus said as they accelerated down Michigan Avenue, on their way to the club.

"I know, I know, but once you see all these bad-ass hoes out here, you'a be thanking me later," Mikey replied, with JR and Pee Wee in the backseat agreeing to his statement.

As Marcus and his entourage behind him pulled up to the club, Marcus demanded the valet to park his truck as close to the club as possible.

The line to the club was wrapped around the corner, filled with beautiful women. By the music that was coming from inside the club and the women that were going in, Marcus and his crew of fifteen guys were anxious to get in.

"Damn, that line long as hell . . . ," JR stated as they stood in front of the club, waiting on everyone else to walk up. "I know we ain't waitin' in that shit?" JR wasn't really the going-out type. He would rather do his job, which consisted of helping Marcus put together all the work and keeping count of all the re-up money.

"Hell Naw . . . ," Marcus replied. "Y'all wait right here while I go holla at whoever' at the door," Marcus said as he walked off toward the entrance, getting all the attention from the women in the line.

After discussing a deal with the bouncer, Marcus was able to get him and his entourage in with no problem. With a wave of a hand, Marcus instructed his crew to follow him inside the club. Once making it inside, instead of mingling with the packed crowd, Marcus and his crew were directed to the upper level where the VIP area was sectioned off with tables and leather sofas. There were two other couples stationed in VIP, but once Marcus and the fifteen others strolled in, it quickly became filled to capacity.

"Aey, homey . . . !" Marcus called for the bouncer while the rest of his team looked through the bulletproof, one-sided glass, lusting over all the beautiful women that they planned on getting with. "Have the waitress bring over fifteen bottles of Moet and ten-fifths of Remy XO. Here, this should take care of us for the rest of the night," Marcus said as he handed the bouncer ten thousand dollars folded up in ten separate rubber band stacks.

Needless to say, Marcus and his crew had blunts rotating throughout the entire VIP to the point where the two other couples eventually left the area. The nice-looking waitress delivered their order, and from that point on the night was starting to look lovely.

"Aey, lord, I'mma 'bout to go get some of these bad-ass hoes to come party with us VIP style, ya dig!" Mikey said in a slick way while holding a bottle of Moet in one hand and smoking a blunt with the other.

114

"Go enjoy ya' self, that's what we here for, ain't it," Marcus stated calmly, holding a glass of champagne in one hand, and the other hand rested on Mikey shoulder.

"You damn right!" Mikey smiled while turning away to leave out of VIP with nine other lords following suit, all of them with bottles of Moet or Remy XO in their hand; Lil G, Pee Wee, and Marlin was included with the group.

Marcus, JR, and a few others stood in VIP, looking down at the crowded club scene while listening to the DJ spin Notorious B.I.G hit record, "One More Chance."

"We came a long ways from running around on the block to where we at now . . . ," Marcus mentioned to JR before taking a sip from his glass. "But I still feel like we got a lot more to do."

JR stood there staring at the club scene for a moment in silence as if he was in meditation. Before facing Marcus, he said, "You know Smitty might choose you to sit in that seat while he gone, right?"

"Why you say that . . . ?" Marcus asked with major concern. "Spoonie the next in line for that slot."

"Smitty took a real liken to you befo' he lef'. He knows Big C and Steve gon' guide you in the right direction . . . ," JR continued to explain intensely. "Spoonie don't have the mind-set to run a nation. Look at him now, out there robbing other vice lord brotha's that's outside the neighborhood. Smitty know if he blessed him wit' chief status, somebody in the nation would whack his ass jus' to see you or one of the other elites in that seat."

JR was the only person out of the crew that Marcus could have logical conversations with about nation business. Marcus stood there, giving JR his undivided attention.

"You ready to be labeled chief of this nation?" JR asked with all seriousness.

Looking JR square in the eyes, he replied, "You know I am." They shook up and then turned their attention back toward the party scene.

Marcus and the others in VIP continued to enjoy themselves. While checking out the crowd, JR spotted Mikey and the others on the dance floor having a good time with some nice-looking females, when he noticed a commotion breaking out between Mikey and an unfamiliar face. Marcus and the other four immediately wrestled their way through the crowded club that consisted of everyone grooving and dancing to the blasting sounds of house music. "It's time for the percolator, it's time for the percolator, it's time for the percolator " . . ." was all you heard pumping out of the club speakers as most people were performing the dance move that went along with the song.

"How the fuck you gon' get mad at me 'cause yo' bitch chose . . . !" Mikey hollered out argumentatively, inches away from the guy's face with the rest of the lords standing behind him. "You better charge that shit to the game, nigga!" These were the words Marcus heard as he began to step in between the two.

"What's goin' on?" Marcus loudly spoke over the music while putting a hand in front of Mikey as he turned to face the dude.

"This hoe-azz nigga act like he wanna do some'nt!" Mikey yelled while forcefully stepping up to the forefront.

"Homey, I ain't worried 'bout you or them niggaz you wit'!" the dude responded, matching Mikey's aggression, obviously showing signs that he had too many drinks.

"Look, dude, don't do that to ya'self," Marcus simply responded, but his expression showed that he meant business. "Now I advise you and ya' mans 'n' nem to go 'head on 'bout y'all bin'nis!"

The three guys that stood beside the dude began grabbing hold of their friend after seeing the stone-cold seriousness upon Marcus's face.

While fiercely pushing against his friends' attempt to pull him away from the scene, he shouted out, "Keisha, bring yo' ma'fuckin' ass here!"

After noticing the sexy young lady not making a move from out of Mikey's embrace, Marcus responded, "Nah, she wit' da team for the night. Now, do we have a problem?!" he said while mean mugging, placing his right hand underneath his linen shirt.

"Come-on, man, fuck that bitch!" one of his friends hollered out as they forcefully began pulling him away.

"A'ight, my nigga, you got it, don't trip!" the dude said while shaking his head in an up-and-down motion before fading away into the crowd.

Most of the attention on that particular side of the club was on the commotion at hand. Mikey noticed all the attention and took advantage of it as he stood up on a nearby stool and shouted the words, "TO ALL THE BEAUTIFUL LADIES IN THE HOUSE. IF Y'ALL WONNA KICK IT WIT' SOME REAL-AZZ NIGGAZ, FOLLOW US TO THE VIP AND LET'S HAVE US A GOOD TIME . . . !" while holding up a half-emptied bottle of Moet in one hand and a fifth of Remy XO in the other.

After Mikey made that display, all the lords cheered him on and wildly began grooving to the loud sounds of Pac's hit record, "Gangsta' Party." The entire crowd got hype! While everyone had their minds set on partying the night out, Marcus kept his eyes on the guys they just had an altercation with until noticing the security aggressively escorting them out the club.

Once making it back to the VIP section, Marcus and his crew had it packed beyond capacity with nothing but thick 'n' sexy females that preferred to party with a bunch of thugged-out-ass niggaz that also knew how to be gentlemen. Of course without any hesitation, Marcus chose two beautiful women to accompany himself with. The remainder of the club night consisted of good smoking and expensive drinking. A great vibe was surrounding the atmosphere. The scene Marcus and his crew had in the VIP really showed the ladies how a real "gangster party" should be conducted.

By the time the DJ announced last call for alcohol, Marcus and his crew had already figured out which females they were going to leave with for an after party, which was usually at someone's home or at a hotel room. Around a quarter 'til four, the dance floor and the rest of the club area was fairly empty before Marcus and his entourage began staggering out the VIP section. Everyone had their pair of females with them while exiting the club. Majority of the crowd were stumbling drunkenly as they walked and talked with amusement. Marcus and JR seemed like the only two out the crew that weren't sloppy drunk. While standing outside the club loudly conversing with each other, the valet was pulling up in their cars one at a time. Marcus noticed a frail guy walking with his head down on the same side of the street as them, wearing all black and a baseball cap that literally covered his eyes. Marcus didn't bother to inform his team on the unusual person that was in the process of walking past the crowd because he didn't want to seem paranoid, and he figured by everyone being strapped with pistols that they were all right. Marcus kept his eyes on the suspicious man until he passed by him. Once recognizing that he wasn't one of the guys that they had a conflict with earlier that night, Marcus went back to conversing with the females that were standing next to him. Moments after turning his attention off the guy, shots rang out! After the first shot was fired, everyone took over panicking, and all the women began screaming hysterically! In the midst of the six shots being fired, Marcus kept a straight head and pulled his pistol while trying to locate where the shooting was coming from. He quickly saw the guy in all black unloading rounds at someone in the crew before rapidly returning shots, causing him to run, scared, off through the dark alleyway that was next to the club. For a split second, everything went silent after the shooting ended, as Marcus was still in his shooting stance while deeply breathing.

"Oh my God!!! Noooooooo!!!" one of the young ladies desperately burst out screaming, breaking the couple seconds of silence.

Everyone ran over to see what horror her eyes had witnessed. And there he was, lying on his back in between two parked cars, choking off his own blood. Right next to him laid a young lady that showed no signs of movement.

"Nawl! Not my ma'fuckin' nigga!" Lil G exclaimed hysterically as he and the others rushed over to aid Mikey.

"Someone get us some help, pleeease!!! We got two people ova' here dying!" a young lady cried out loudly to no one in particular.

Everyone was trying their best to help the two, but it was obvious that the young lady was not breathing. Instead of waiting for help, Marcus took matters into his own hands. He and the rest of the crew carefully picked Mikey up and rushed him to the nearest emergency room.

Chapter 16

"Chris!" Sylvia yelled from the bedroom, attempting to get her son's attention.

"Huh!" Chris replied while giving his undivided attention to the PlayStation's NBA Live '95 that was displayed on the floor model television, located in their living room.

"Don't huh me! Get cha' mind out that damn game and come're for a second!"

"Ugggghh!" Chris gave a long sigh before setting the game on pause and reluctantly walking his way toward his mother's bedroom.

"Wassup, Ma?" Chris asked with an irritable tone and expression on his face.

"I need you to run to the store for me."

"Why you ain't ask Daddy? He lying right next to you."

"'Cause that's what we got'chu for," Steve abruptly interfered while lying on his back, controlling the channels on the television. "Now quit giving your momma all that lip and do what she asks."

He been getting' on my gaddamn nerves since he been staying home lately, Chris thought to himself as he listened to his mother's order with his hand out to collect the money. To Chris's surprise, Steve responded, "I read minds too, so you better watch it."

Chris stood there stunned with his mouth half opened, staring at his father. He looked as if his ole man actually knew what his previous thoughts were.

The second Chris stepped foot outside onto the front steps, he inhaled the excruciating heat from the ninety-degree summer afternoon.

"Damn, it's hot as hell out here," Chris mumbled to himself in an unspirited way as he proceeded down the steps. Even though Chris had on a Nike tank top and a pair of basketball shorts, to no avail, the humidity made him feel like he was fully dressed. As Chris strolled his way down Hamlin, on his way to the Arab-owned corner store on Nineteenth and Pulaski, he noticed that the block was fairly empty, with the exception of a few young girls playing double Dutch and a couple of kids riding their bikes. Before making it to the corner of his block, a voice came out of nowhere from afar.

"Chris! Wassup, Jo!" A young voice yelled from one of the houses in the middle of the block.

Chris stopped in his tracks and turned to see who was calling his name. After squinting his eyes to get a location on where the voice was coming from, he recognized it to be Bernard Jackson a.k.a. "Bae Bae."

"Slow up!" Bae Bae insisted while racing down his front steps heading in Chris's direction.

"Where you on yo' way to?" Bae Bae asked, inching closer toward Chris's presence.

"Fenna' walk up here to the store for Moms 'n' shit. Wassup?"

"I'll walk up there wit'chú," Bae Bae said as they shook up with each other and went about their journey.

On their walk to the store they made a lot of small talk about what had been going on in the neighborhood and also witnessing the "slick boyz" harassing some young hustlaz along Nineteenth Street.

"They always fuckin' wit' somebody," Bae Bae complained as they passed a normal scene of dirty detectives stretching out a few teenagers along the side of a building. "Muthafuckas ain't got shit better else to do," he mumbled while staring at the action.

As they continued to walk, Bae Bae interrupted their attention from the police activity by blurting out, "Aey, Chris, you ain't decided what high school you wanna play for. I know you been getting a lot of letters from different schools 'n' shit."

"Hell naw. I kno' I'm tired of this Catholic school bullshit. Gotta wear uniforms 'n' shit and follow all them stupid-ass rules. All the letters I got been from all-boy Catholic schools!" Chris explained.

"Aw, hell naw!" Bae Bae expressed dramatically with disbelief. "No hoes? I couldn't do that shit!"

"I know, man, I ain't feeling that shit either. That's why I ain't chosen a school to go to, yet."

"Thats all I'm tryn'a do when I start high school is fuck all the hoes and make my name known all ova' that ma'fucka," Bae Bae expressed himself in an eagerly fashion while easing a half-smoked blunt from out of his pocket with a lighter. "You wanna hit this shit?" he asked with a mischievous grin on his face.

"Nawl, I'm straight."

"You sho'! This that good shit your brotha' 'nem got ova' there on Avers," Bae Bae said, trying to sound convincing.

"Gon' 'head 'n' get high, I'm good," Chris insisted.

Bae Bae was the type of kid that was destined for destruction. He lived a few doors down from Chris and lived under some of the same scenarios that most teens were faced with in most 'hoods, the lack of good parental guidance. Even though Chris experienced smoking weed before with a few of his teammates, he refused to expose that side of him to Bae Bae; besides, they weren't even close friends. By the time they made it to the store, Bae Bae had already saw a group of young guys from the area to follow up behind, which looked more of his type of crowd.

On their ecstatic trip to the nearest hospital, everyone that jumped in the car with Marcus was trying their best to keep Mikey resuscitated. By the time they arrived at the emergency room and rushed Mikey in on a stretcher, he was still fighting for his life as he attempted to take deep breaths while blood consistently pumped from his mouth and blood also filled his clothing. Marcus and the rest of the crew, followed by a few others, sat patiently in the waiting room while the doctors operated on Mikey in the intensive care unit.

"Is the family of a Michael Robinson present?" A tall slender white surgeon with surgical equipment as his attire asked as he stepped foot inside the waiting room.

"Yeah. That's my ma'fuckin' cousin!" Lil G snapped as they all stood up with dried-up bloodstains covering their clothing.

"Well, is there any immediate family available? As far as a mother, father, brother—"

"What'chú sayin', Doc!" Lil G angrily interrupted the doctor's statement as he began to approach him with aggression until everyone held him back. "We all the family you need to be talkin' to right now!" Lil G stated emotionally with his voice on the verge of cracking and his eyes seconds away from being filled with tears.

"What I'm saying is," The doctor hesitated with a slight annoyance. "After several attempts of trying to revive Mr. Robinson, I'm afraid a main artery was hit that caused a tremendous loss of blood. I'm sorry but—"

Before the doctor was able to finish his statement, the room went up in a horrific roar! The doctor's body language told it all after mentioning the damage done to the main artery. From that point on, everyone in the room sensed the bad news.

At approximately 5:03 a.m. early Sunday morning, Michael D. Robinson a.k.a. "Mikey" was pronounced dead in the emergency room of St. Francis Medical Center, ten minutes away from the club.

"I don't usually meet this nigga out at his crib, but once I told him 'bout'chu and what we tryn'a do, he definitely wanted to meet up. It helped that I mentioned we had enough paper to grab two keys," Shawn conversed with Marcus as they drove on Interstate 80 expressway heading toward the far south suburbs to Shawn's connect. Majority of the ride, Marcus was quiet while listening to Shawn explain the situation. It was obvious that something was bothering Marcus because he barely commented on anything Shawn was saying.

"Y'all still ain't found out who did that shit, huh?" Shawn asked with great concern, referring to the unsolved murder of Mikey, sensing what was going through Marcus's mind.

Marcus answered with a simple nod of the head that indicated no. It ate him up inside that they weren't able to retaliate on anyone specifically, especially after seeing how devastated Mikey's family was at the funeral a week earlier. Shawn showed up at the funeral to pay his respects, so he witnessed how hysterically the women of the family were crying and how Marcus and the rest of the crew were trying their best to console his mother and three sisters. The stale expressions on the crew and other vice lord brothers' faces showed revenge, but everyone was helpless without a lead to who had done it and where it came from.

"What'chú say this nigga name was again?" Marcus asked, obviously changing subjects.

"We call'em Kunta. He'a black-ass nigga from Nigeria," Shawn began to explain. "He coola' than a fan and he's a loyal ma'fucka too."

"Oh yea," Marcus simply replied as he began to fill an empty Phillies blunt with some lime green reefer.

All that was going through Marcus's mind was a consistent heroin connect of his own that he could not only use with Shawn but also use to supply half the west side, if the product was as good as Shawn claimed.

After a forty-five-minute trip from the west side to the far south suburbs, Shawn finally exited off of 183rd Street and made a quick right onto Pulaski Rd, that led him directly to Kunta two level all brick estate. They drove along the Spiral drive way that led them toward his four-car garage. Real millionaire status shit!

"Gaaaddamn! This nigga gettin' it, ain't he?" Marcus exclaimed.

"Yea, he better be, how much money we been bringing him ova' the years," Shawn responded.

As they exited from Shawn's BMW, heading toward the front entrance of Kunta's empire, they were admiring everything the home had to offer—from its water fountain statue in the front yard, all the way to the indoor/outdoor Olympic-style swimming pool in the backyard. Approaching the front-door steps, they noticed a huge crystal chandelier hanging from the high ceiling, which had them mesmerized. Shawn was inches away from pressing the doorbell when the front door slowly began to open.

"Welcome!" a beautiful dark-skinned woman that looked to be in her early forties opened the door with open arms.

"Thank you. How you been doing, Mofie?" Shawn asked, acknowledging the woman with a half hug and a formal peck on the cheek.

"I've been making it, Shawn, how about you?" Mofie asked in her strong African accent as she rested her hand on Shawn's shoulder.

"Same here, same here," Shawn replied while turning his attention to introducing Marcus. "Mofie, this is my best friend Marcus. Marcus, this Kunta's beautiful wife, Mofie."

"Nice to meet you," Marcus said, reaching out for her hand. Marcus was temporarily startled at the different decorations that filled the main floor. The walls were covered with expensive African paintings, and different kinds of unique sculptures were throughout the entire area.

After greeting Marcus, she stated, "Well, let's not prolong this matter any longer. That husband of mine been expecting you, gentlemen. This way, shall we?" Mofie began to lead them down a long hallway to where Kunta was stationed. They walked up to a room door that had the word "private" engraved inside the fine wood grain. "Honey, your guests have arrived," Mofie informed in an elegant fashion after three light knocks at the door.

"Come-on in," The voice from inside the room demanded.

As they made their entrance, the room was noticeably Kunta's office space. Kunta sat in a plush maroon leather rocking chair behind a huge cherry oak wood desk with four security cameras that sat counter corner on top of the desk, showing all sections of his home.

"Shawn! My main man!" Kunta greeted his company proudly with open arms. "What's goin' on, my brother!" he said in his strong foreign accent while walking up to embrace Shawn with both arms.

"Nuttin' much, Kunta. Same ole shit, different toilet, ya kno'," Shawn replied with a gracious grin on his face, still shaking hands with Kunta.

In the same notion, Kunta glanced over at Marcus. "And I take it this must be the infamous Marcus," he said while turning his attention toward Marcus. Marcus raised one eyebrow at the comment.

"Honey, did you need me to bring you guys anything before I leave?" Mofie kindly interrupted.

"As a matter of fact, you sure can," Kunta assured. "Bring me the usual. You boys don't mind having a shot or two with me, do ya?" Kunta asked with a curious smirk on his face.

"Not at all," Shawn answered for the both of them.

While Kunta's wife was gone to fulfill his wishes, the three of them continued to make small conversation. Marcus was being more observant, while Shawn seemed to be comfortable as if he was amongst family. In Marcus's eyes, Kunta seemed like the smooth businessman type. Despite Kunta's strong accent, he still had a sense of humor. It was obvious that he'd been around some brothers from the streets by the way he conducted himself.

Ten minutes later, his wife arrived with some expensive tequila along with three shot glasses.

"Thank you, sweetie. That'll be it for now," Kunta said as he dismissed his wife with a nod of the head.

As Kunta began to pour the liquor in the shot glasses, the mood of their conversation gradually turned more into serious business talk than their previous "getting acquainted with each other" conversation.

"Sooooo . . . Ya' uncle tells me you tryn'a start your own operation," Kunta announced in the midst of handing them their shot glasses.

"Well, I'm jus' looking for a little more independence. Besides, my family is focusing more on that new construction company we're tryn'a get off the ground," Shawn said before the

126

three of them gulped the shots of tequila at the same time. Shawn talked with much sense to be a twenty-two-year-old hustler.

"Construction! Legal and you can earn great money. Why not choose that path!" Kunta spoke in broken English with his heavy accent, showing signs of concern for Shawn's well-being.

"Later on down the line, maybe. But right now I have a master plan that I want to put together so I can get one good run in," Shawn expressed himself with confidence.

"One good run, huh! Well, I hope so 'cause this is it for me, Shawn, "Kunta replied while pouring another round of tequila shots. "I made good over the years, and it's only so long before things could start going wrong."

As everyone threw back their second shot of tequila, Kunta turned his attention to Marcus as he sat his glass down on his desk.

"So, what about you? What're you gonna do after this is over?" Kunta asked, staring Marcus directly in the eyes with his bloodshot-colored eyes.

"Well, I have a few things up my sleeve," Marcus answered, not really knowing what to say at the time.

"I don't know if Shawn told you, but him and his uncles are family to me. They're like my brothers! Now that he brought you around, I look at you the same way, unless you show me otherwise," Kunta explained himself with different hand gestures.

Marcus gave his undivided attention while Kunta continued to express his feelings toward Shawn's family and the hustling game. Marcus, feeling tremendous warmth from the liquor, stayed focused with the discussion because he knew they were on to something big. After everything was said and done, Kunta stated, "Shawn!" He spoke loudly, obviously feeling the liquor as well. "Within five years, I'm wiping my slate clean. I have too much going for myself to get caught up, ya kno'! And I have some great investment opportunities that I'm gonna put you young brothers on so that both of you could do the same. All I ask for is . . . loyalty!" Kunta lectured while glancing at them both eye to eye in his most serious mug.

Before they left Kunta's presence, he gave them two grams of hard cocoa brown raw heroin to put a mix on so they could give samples to some dope fiends to check the potency. He instructed them to hit the dope with no more than ten Dormin pills, even though it was able to stand up to at least twenty-five pills. The less mix, the stronger the product. The more mix stretches the dope further, and it still would be very good, but it wouldn't be the best in the city like Shawn and Marcus were eager to have. Marcus left feeling real good about the situation and was anxious to get it going.

Chapter 17

A week after the meeting with Kunta, Marcus and Shawn met up with one of Kunta's runners at a neutral location to do business. The samples that they were given were everything they wanted and more. After putting the mix that Kunta suggested, Marcus went to some of the hardest dope fiends in the Holy City while Shawn stayed around Division area, giving fiends a sample of the blows (heroin) that they were going to have out on the streets. The reactions they were getting were phenomenal for what they were trying to do. Some of the hypes that shot up dope, which gets to main stream quicker, know most definitely, if the drug was potent or not immediately. Marcus asked one of his hard-to-satisfy shooters on a scale from one to ten, how would he rate the dope? When he was able to talk and focus, he told him a twenty and asked when and where they were going to open up shop! From that point, Marcus knew they had a winner and was anxious to put it out in the streets. Before any of the real hustlers opened up a big-time heroin joint (spot), they would always do major "pass-outs" on the block where the drugs were sold so the customers would know what they were getting; usually if the dope was a bomb, they'd come right back to purchase more. If you had excellent dope, this strategy was the key to success.

While sitting at the table in one of Shawn's low-key, unoccupied apartments, Marcus and Shawn separated two keys of raw heroin into all grams. Kunta was willing to give them whatever they needed on consignment, but Marcus insisted on them purchasing their own product. After paying fifty thousand for a thousand grams, which was equivalent to a kilo, Marcus was getting a cheaper price than he was used to. Kunta still ended up fronting them an extra key.

"How that muthafucka reacted yesterday. I kno' this shit gotta be a bomb!" Shawn eagerly said while in the process of laying out large square pieces of extra-heavy-duty aluminum foil across the living room glass table.

"Hell yea," Marcus mildly replied while crushing a hundred grams of raw dope into dust particles, preparing to mix it together with the dormin pills. After putting the mix with the dope, he then put it all in a Mr. Coffee grinder, which was usually used to grind coffee beans, to make a fine blend. As Marcus pressed on the top of the machine to make it operate, he then shook it in an up-and-down motion repeatedly to make sure he got a proper mix.

After about ten minutes of shaking the dope, Marcus looked up at Shawn with a mischievous grin before taking the lid off and stating, "This is it, my nigga, the beginning of a ma'fuckin' empire." When he took the top off the blender, it let out a thick puff of smoke that had a loud vinegar smell, which usually indicates a sign of great potency.

A couple of hours into putting in work at the table, Marcus ignored a few calls that seemed to have bothered his focus. After the fourth consecutive unanswered call, Marcus finally answered with a slight attitude, "Hello!"

"Damn, this what I gotta go through to holla' at'chú?" The familiar masculine voice on the other end spoke.

Knowing that it was Spoonie on the phone really annoyed Marcus at that moment, and he showed a disgusted expression once Spoonie made that statement.

"Aey, I'm busy right now let me hit'chu back in'a minute, Jo."

"its sho'll funny how you always busy and we out here fucked up in'a drought," Spoonie said sarcastically in an evil-spirited tone.

Before responding to his statement, Marcus looked at his phone with a strange expression.

"Everything gon' be a'ight in'a minute. Wassup though?" Marcus replied calmly, obviously trying hard to keep his composure. Even though Marcus may have surpassed Spoonie in the money department due to him being a bit more business savvy, Spoonie was still ranked higher than him with a five-star universal status. Marcus hadn't been showing any signs of honoring Spoonie position since Smitty left the streets. He even ignored a couple of meetings that Spoonie called amongst the IVLN, which was something he never did when Smitty was on the streets.

"Chief wants all the elites to meet up on Twenty-first Friday around seven. That's if you ain't too busy," Spoonie mentioned, taking another crack at Marcus.

"He must know how much time they're tryn'a give him?"

"More than likely he gon' let it be known who's in charge of the entire nation's business. If you ask me, he should've been done that so we could get back to work. Everybody should already know who's next to being chief," Spoonie said in an arrogant fashion, making references to himself as being the next chief of the IVLs.

"A'ight, I'll make sho' me and my team be there," Marcus said before ending the call.

Marcus didn't know what to make out of the conversation between him and Spoonie, but whatever decisions that were about to be made amongst the nation weren't going to interfere with what he and Shawn had in the making on the other side of town.

Before passing out dope samples to the fiends from around Division and other surrounding blocks, Marcus and Shawn made sure to secure their joint (spot), which was a sixteen-unit, four-story co-way building on the corner of Menard and Division. They had one of the Shorty lords, from out of Marcus's crew; post up in front of the cabstand to direct all the traffic to the specific floor where the dope was being sold that particular day. The day before, they spreaded the word throughout the entire land that it was going to be a pass-out from 7:00 a.m. to 9:00

A.m. anytime after nine, the customers would have to come with a dub (twenty dollars).

As you could imagine, at ten minutes 'til seven, the building had a line wrapped around the corner with fiends anxious to receive free dope.

"Where that dope at!"

"Who got the blows, Shorty!" A couple of hypes muttered while staggering up frantically.

"Y'all better get some order and make a line or ain't nobody getting shit!" The young lord demanded fiercely in the midst of all the commotion.

As the fiends began to flood the building by walking up in groups and some pulling up in cars, the Shorty started sending them to the lobby of the building by the tens while another Shorty frisked everyone down before directing them to the floor where the blows were being passed out that particular day.

Throughout the entire ordeal, Marcus and Shawn sat patiently in a low-key car with jet-black tint that was parked on Menard, where they were able to witness how their operation was being handled and how the customers reacted to the product. Previous to the pass-out, Marcus and Shawn had designed the setup to perfection, so all the workers and security had to do was play their position properly. Before it was all said and done, a hundred blows were passed out to a hundred different customers within thirty minutes. For the remainder of the pass-out time, the people that received free blows had to pay if they came back for more.

By the end of the day, $2,000 worth of blows was passed out and five g-bundles ($5,000) were sold, which was good for the opening day. This was a great sign of a successful joint!

Cars were lined up along Twenty-first Strip as if a car show was in progress. Everybody from the elites down to the pack runners was present on Twenty-first Strip to get the word on Chief Smitty statements. Everyone out there was affiliated with the mob, but they all stood separately within their own branch of lords. Marcus and his crew circled the block twice before finding parks. Marcus walked in the middle of his personal crew as they marched down Twenty-first. At least twenty guys barricaded around Marcus as if they were his personal shield. On their walk down the strip, they passed by nearly two hundred IVLs and even stopped on several occasions to talk with other elites and their crews before making it to the corner of St. Louis and Twenty-first where Big C (chief over the conservatives), Spoonie, Steve, and a few elites from both sides stood in a circle. Marcus noticed a vast majority of the people wore their personally made RIP "Mikey" shirts, paying their respects to a fallen IVL soldier. The environment felt more like a family reunion how everyone was mingling with the brothers they haven't seen in a while.

"Wassup, ole man?" Marcus smiled while greeting Steve with a handshake and a half hug as he approached their circle.

"You wassup. Why you ain't been by the crib lately?" Steve asked, sounding more like a concerned parent, pretending as if he was getting on Marcus's case.

"I was jus' over there the other day hollin' at Momma and Chris. They told me you had jus' stepped out for a minute. Then when they mentioned Big C was back in town, I knew what time it was . . . ," Marcus claimed as he casually turned his attention toward Big C. "Wassup, Unc?" Marcus said, greeting Big C the same way as he did Steve. Coming up in age, Marcus always looked at Big C as an uncle figure because of the closeness between him and Steve, which they had over the years; he also admired how Big C controlled the mob.

"Wassup with'chu, baby!" Big C responded in a slick manner as he embraced Marcus.

"I can't call it, Chief, what's good?"

"You ready?" Big C suddenly asked with a mysterious grin covering his face.

"Ready?" Marcus replied while looking slightly puzzled as if the sudden question caught him off guard. "We stay ready," Marcus stated with more seriousness and confidence but still not knowing what was behind the question.

"A'ight, I'm jus' asking," Big C smoothly retorted.

Marcus then acknowledged everyone else that was posted up in their circle. When it came time to acknowledge Spoonie, they embraced each other halfheartedly. After shaking up, Spoonie blurted out, "Glad you was able to make it."

Marcus ignored the smart comment made by Spoonie; after a couple of seconds of awkward silence in the circle, Big C stated, "All we waiting on is for Smitty to hit the phone and give word on his situation and see who he wanna leave in control of the nation. Of course whatever decisions that are made I'm behind a hundred percent. We all a family."

Big C was one of the long-lasting chiefs of any vice lord organization. The founding fathers and the few before him either died prematurely or were in jail for the remainder of their lives. The conservatives were one of the first movements established amongst the vice lord nation in the early sixties. All other branches came about when leaders in other neighborhoods started their own mobs within the nation. Big C was around as a youngster and was groomed by the founders that laid down the literature and laws for the nation. He and a selective few were legitimate overseers for the entire VL nation, despite everyone doing their own thing within' their respected mobs. The same laws and it had to be followed by everyone. If for any reason the laws were being violated by any leader of any branch of the vice lords, Big C and a few other originals had the power to demote or replace their position.

After several minutes of everyone talking within their crews on Twenty-first, Big C received an expected call at 7:30 p.m. sharp.

"Yeah!" Big C answered on the first ring.

"Hey! wassup!" Smitty spoke through the receiver enthusiastically.

"Jus' was waiting on you. Where you calling from?" Big C asked, trying to make sure it wasn't a direct call from the feds.

"Everything good," Smitty replied, secretly reassuring Big C that the lines were safe to talk on. "Was everybody able to make it?"

"All the important ones. They all standing right next to me," Big C said while attempting to put the phone on speaker.

"Yeah, man, me and my lawyers came to a conclusion and decided to take what they're tryn'a gimme."

"Smith, I got'chu on speakerphone so everybody around me can hear you," Big C said, calling Smitty by his last name.

"Good, good . . . Yeah, they tryn'a offer me a straight ten. The only reason I'mma jump on it 'cause it's gonna be tough tryn'a beat these people in a trial when they got all kinds of secret informants working for them that nobody knows about," Smitty noted suspiciously. "Where my five key playas at?"

"We right here listenin'," All the elites spoke at once.

"I was a little worried 'bout'chu since ain't nobody heard from you in'a few months," Spoonie initiated, making sure his voice was distinguished out from everyone else's.

"I jus' had to get this case behind me so we all could move on. Now that it's out the way, I'mma need y'all more than ever while I'm gone."

"Whatever' business that you need took care of, consider it done!" Spoonie eagerly stated, trying to show signs of leadership.

"Yeah, that's the thing, I need business took care of the right way. I don't need unnecessary wars getting kicked off and I definitely don't need other brotha's into it wit' one another. I need my next leader to not only hold the mob down while I'm gone, but I also need him to take the nation to a higher level."

The crowd around Big C was in complete silence while Smitty was reciting his expectations. In the midst of Smitty speech, everyone that stood out on Twenty-first Strip (which was close to five hundred lords) gradually made their way to the circle to hear Smitty speak.

After a few more demands and instructions to his elites, it finally came time to sanction a new leader to sit in Smitty seat.

"So with all that said, I decided to choose a leader that's a thinker as well as an enforcer . . . ," Smitty continued to explain. "After a few months of thinking and weighing out all options, me and a few other original heads of the nations decided to bless none other than . . . ," he paused before finishing his power statement. "Where ya at, Marcus?!"

The entire crowd that stood out on Twenty-first looked around at each other in awe. Some even showed signs of excitement at the decision that was made. As you could imagine,

Spoonie and the lords that he personally had control over showed no signs of excitement, In fact, Spoonie did everything in his powers to hold back the disgusted feelings that electrified him. With Spoonie having five stars and all the work he personally put in for Smitty, he felt it was a given that he was next in line if anything happened to the chief.

While everyone in the circle was proudly congratulating Marcus as their active chief, Spoonie demeanor showed a definite sign of displeasure toward the decision. When it came time for Marcus to face Big C and Steve, they looked upon him as if they were the proudest father and uncle figures in the world.

After about a minute of Smitty being silent on the phone, he interrupted the mini-celebration by stating, "A'ight! A'ight! Everybody settle down. I ain't got long before this call ends. Now I didn't make that decision to step on anyone's toes." Smitty said this speaking to Spoonie in particular.

Spoonie looked on with a stale expression as if a major thought was rambling through his brain. "The decision was based on what was best for the nation as a whole," Smitty went on to explain. "Spoonie, I need you to keep doing what you do without all the negative attention. Even though I won't be present, any orders and commands would still come from me through the wire." Before ending his conversation, Smitty blurted out, "Aey, Marcus!"

"I'm right here, Chief. Talk to me!" Marcus responded graciously.

"I know this is a big step for you. I'm investing a lot into you. Now is the time to let it be known if you'a be able to handle this shit or not!" he said with meaning and emphasis behind every word.

Before answering, Marcus slowly glanced through the entire crowd, seeing a majority of proud faces, while having flashbacks of his life from when it all started, all the way to his present situation.

"Yeah . . . yeah, I'm ready, Chief!" Marcus claimed while staring at Big C, finally understanding the meaning behind Big C's earlier question ("You ready?").

Chapter 18

Despite a few shoot-outs with some hating Four Corner Hustlaz around Division and a couple of mishaps with the stickup men, the spot on Menard was moving beyond Marcus's expectations. Within a month's time, Marcus and Shawn had the building on Menard operating like a real 'cartel,' how they had customers flowing in and out twenty-four hours, seven days a week. The Division area wasn't used to seeing this much action every day of the week before Marcus brought his hustling ways around the area. Even though the twins, Dre and Drew, was getting rich and had shit on smash around Division, Marcus and Shawn had some heroin that no other hustler in the area could stand up to. They climbed the ladder of success pretty quickly by staying consistent with great product and treating their customers well. From the time they had a pass-out, they went from making five thousand a day to anywhere from thirty to forty thousand a day off of dimes and dubs. Prior to opening up their spot, Shawn came to terms with the twins that they would only sell heroin while the twins continued to sale crack. Most dope fiends that snort blows usually need a rock to follow the dope to enhance their high. So it was safe to say, by the dope selling so good, it put extra dollars in the twins' pockets, which was all good with the twins, but other higher-ranked officials in the Four Corner Hustlers mob didn't agree.

It had been nearly a month since Marcus was blessed with chief status. He definitely was moving differently in the streets; he rarely was seen joyriding through the streets of Chicago. He always kept a selected few with him at all times, which was Pee Wee and Marlin, two of his main go-getters. Since they had the joint on Menard off the ground, he began focusing on restoring the blocks in the Holy City. This was a good thing as well as a bad thing because without Marcus being around Division as much, it left some doors open for certain conflicts to indulge on their operation, not to mention that all vice lords from out of the Holy City were running a joint in an all–Four Corner Hustler 'hood.

As Shawn proceeded to exit off the Austin Boulevard ramp, he began dialing a number to one of the Shorty lords who was running the afternoon shift on Menard.

"Yeah!" announced a male in an aggressive tone.

"Aey, I'm gettin' off at Austin right now. I should be pullin' up in about ten, fifteen minutes."

"About time, these muthafuckas gettin' real impatient."

"Next time don't wait 'til y'all dry before callin' me! You know them people be needin' that shit."

"A'ight, jus' hurry up, big homey. We got'a fuckin' soup line out here!" The young hustler said, continuing to talk recklessly over the phone.

Before Shawn was able to end the call with one of the pack runners, his other line beeped.

"A'ight, I'll be there in'a minute, let me catch this other line real quick."

"Hello!" Shawn answered without noticing the number.

"Wassup, foe!" The voice on the other end spoke.

"Yeah, wassup, who this?"

"This Dre, nigga. Where ya at?"

"Heading toward Division. 'Bout to handle some'nt."

"Call me when you get around, I need to bump heads wit'chú, it's important."

"A'ight. Everything cool?" Shawn asked with concern.

"I don't know, we'll see in'a minute," Dre, one of the twins, said suspiciously.

138

Once ending the call, Shawn was trying to figure out what was the sudden meet-up about. He wasn't too worried because everything was set in stone with him and the twins.

After taking care of business, dropping off ten g-bundles to a Shorty, Shawn met up with Dre outside the building on Menard. To his surprise, Dre was accompanied by the prince of the 4CH's, B-lo. B-lo was the leader over all foe's, one step under King Rodney. B-lo was a treacherous leader and whenever he came around it had to be something major going on in their territory. The moment Shawn witnessed them both exit the car, he instantly got bubble guts, not knowing what to expect from the two.

"Wassup, foe!" B-lo greeted Shawn aggressively with their nation's handshake as they approached each other in front of the cabstand.

"Prince Lo, what's good?" Shawn replied with his eyes filled with intimidation. B-lo had this effect on just about anybody, with his six-three, two-hundred-seventy-pound stance and a facial expression that kept a permanent frown.

"You, that's what's good, I hear you and that hook-azz nigga ova' here doin' y'all thang!"

"We doing a'ight," Shawn said reluctantly.

"A'ight?" B-lo questioned with a strange look upon his face. "Word on the street is that you muthafuckas pullin' in damn near forty thousand a day!"

Shawn simply shrugged his shoulders, not really having a response to B-lo's statement because it was the truth.

"I mean, I ain't got no problem wit'chú gettin' some paper on the land, but it seem like you ain't tryn'a fuck wit' the foe's at all and I jus' think that it's time for you and dat nigga to start paying homage!"

After a split second of silence, Shawn replied, "I'm sure somethin' can be worked out. What we talkin'?" Shawn pleaded, feeling more than helpless at that moment.

"I don't know about twin, but I'mma need'a light," B-lo hesitated as if he was thinking of a figure in his head. "Let's say fifty stacks."

139

Shawn stood there emotionlessly and puzzled from the situation at hand. There was no way possible that he could have left the scene without agreeing to all of Prince B-lo's terms.

"Awe yea, I wouldn't mind having contact with that connect who you getting that fire-ass dope from, either. And for future references, get them niggaz off our land, including that nigga Marcus," B-lo continued to instruct Shawn. "I really should be getting on the twins' ass for allowing this shit to go down."

Dre stood there the entire time in silence. He really didn't have a problem with Marcus and the other lords, but it was way over his head now. Even though Shawn's uncles had juice amongst the foes, their rank was held in another 'hood and Prince B-lo was over their heads too. "So, I'mma give you and Marcus by the end of the week to come up wit' what I need, understood?"

Shawn simply nodded his head in agreement, but what was really going through his mind was trouble. He knew once he informed Marcus about the situation, it was going to be a problem, especially now that Marcus was a chief.

Before walking off, B-lo stated, "Cheer up, baby, it's all good. There's still a lot of money to be made." He said this as they shook up.

While B-lo and Dre walked off toward the car, Shawn stood there until they pulled off. Once they drove out of eyesight, Shawn instantly began dialing numbers on his cell phone.

"Hello," the voice on the other end spoke in a bored tone.

"Wassup, homey. Aey look, I need to holla' at'chú. We got'a problem on our hands that needs to get dealt with."

"Okay, I'll get wit'chú a little later on," Marcus simply replied.

Since the meeting with Kunta, the Nigerian dope connect, Marcus escalated his relationship with him tremendously. Now that Marcus was sitting in the highest seat for the IVLs, he had an entire mob to supply. Even though Big C had his own connections, he couldn't resist going through Marcus to get his supply of heroin due to the fact that the potency of the product was rare. Marcus was getting keys of heroin for thirty thousand, the cheapest anyone in the city could have possibly gotten it for unless they traveled outside the States, and that was very unlikely. Every week Marcus had a high demand of twenty keys of heroin to distribute, which was way more than Kunta bargained for. Ten went to Big C, five for the spot on Menard, and the other five keys were separated into grams for the elites to feed the land that they were in charge over. Since Marcus was getting it for so cheap, he had room to put taxes on his price tag and still would have the most competitive prices in the city. He charged Big C ten thousand more than what he was paying for a key. All the elites that were over a particular area, he fronted however many grams they needed for sixty dollars a gram, which was a far better price tag than they were getting when Smitty was in the seat. Marcus was making a pretty nice profit off just dealing weight alone, but he was beginning to make an even bigger fortune off the growing spot on Menard and Division.

On a very seldom day of driving around different areas in the city where the IVLs dwelled, Marcus passed through Avers Street, where he allowed Lil G to reopen the block and have complete control over it. Of course Marcus kept him supplied with the best product, but since Marcus wasn't hands-on with the block anymore, for some reason Avers wasn't making the same type of money. Avers went from bringing in twenty thousand a day to now making anywhere from two to five stacks a day. Part of the reason for the decline was because of the surrounding blocks that had dope that was just as good, all sponsored by Marcus, and the lack of discipline.

Marcus and Pee Wee pulled up on Avers in his blue '96 Suburban with Pee Wee driving. The truck had jet-black tint on every window, so in order to be seen, the windows had to be let down.

"Wudd up, lord!" Lil G hollered out while pursuing the truck. "Jus' the person I needed to see!" he said once noticing Marcus.

"Jump in and ride wit' me so we can holla'."

Before getting all the way in the car, Lil G instructed one of the shortys on what he needed done while he was gone.

They drove through the surrounding blocks so Marcus could check on things in the area when lil G blurted out, "Aey, lord, it's been slow than'a muthafucka for me the last couple days." He continued to state, "My customers been telling me somebody opened up down here on Lawndale."

"Shouldn't nobody be working on Lawndale," Marcus calmly replied while being carefully observant of the blocks they drove through.

"Spoonie the only person close to you I gave some dope to and he got his guys working the Twenty-first Strip."

"Let's ride through Lawndale. I bet'chu we see some ma'fuckas out there working!" Lil G claimed as they accelerated a few blocks down Cermak. Lawndale was only a four-block radius from Avers Street. Once making it to the block, true enough they witnessed a steady flow of traffic; fiends frantically walking up with cash in hand, cars holding up traffic in the middle of the block, Shorty lords ripping back and forth, rotating packs—all signs of a booming joint!

"Damn!" Marcus inadvertently blurted out. "You what'nt bullshittin', huh? Who that is standing over there on'a phone like he runnin' some shit!" he said in an uneasy tone as they slowly exited down Lawndale.

"That's Spoonie cousin," Lil G answered while they yielded behind a car, with someone excitedly hollering back and forth with Spoonie cousin who stood on the sidewalk. "The nigga name Peanut. He one of them New Breeds from out of K-Town."

As soon as Lil G mentioned "New Breed," it instantly struck a nerve inside of Marcus. Not only was the opposition hustling on Vice Lord land, but to make matters worse, Marcus didn't give permission, and his right-hand man's toes were being stepped on. After the traffic cleared up and Marcus was able to pull closer to Peanut's presence, he shouted out the window, "Aey, let me holla' at'chu real quick."

"Get out and holla' then!" Peanut replied arrogantly.

"What!" Pee Wee reacted dramatically while instinctively grabbing hold of the handle of his pistol resting on his waistline. Marcus stopped Pee Wee in his tracks before he could let another word out.

142

"You right. Don't go nowhere, let us catch'a park real quick," Marcus calmly shouted out to Peanut as they swerved into the nearest park.

When Marcus and his two comrades got out approaching Peanut, he continued on with his phone conversation as if Marcus was some type of small-time street punk.

"Who put some work on this block?" Marcus boldly asked Peanut as they faced off.

"Let me call you right back," Peanut said through the phone receiver. "What is it to you?" he replied in a cocky manner.

Marcus again had to restrain his guys from making a move against Peanut for being disrespectful.

"What is it to me?" Marcus said in disbelief. "Do you know who the fuck I am?!"

The shortys that gathered around the commotion felt the drama rising in the air once Marcus made that comment. They began to scatter away from the crowd, scared.

"Yeah, I know who you supposed to be. To my knowledge, my cousin runnin' this sh—"

Smack! Was the loud sound that was heard from Marcus's open hand landing fiercely on the jaw of Peanut before he was able to finish his statement. In the same motion, Marcus untucked his .9mm and muscled it in Peanut's mouth.

"Listen here, muthafucka . . . !" Marcus aggressively spoke in a devilish tone. "Whoever gave you the green light to work over here steered you in the wrong direction. Now I advise you to get the fuck out'a dodge if you wanna live!" With one hand gripped around Peanut's throat and the other with the pistol positioned in his mouth, Peanut still managed to show no signs of fear while coldly staring Marcus directly in the eyes.

In the midst of Marcus handling the situation, Lil G and Pee Wee had their pistols untucked in hand when Lil G yelled out to the lords on the block, "Whoever got the rest of this work better gimme that shit right now or a'ma'fucka getting violated!" Once that was said, the Shorty that was running the block immediately ran up and dropped the remaining of the blows in Lil G's hands and demanded one of the other shortys to get the other packs from the hidden stash spot on the block.

With the pistol still rested in Peanut's mouth, Marcus aggressively stated, "Muthafucka, you got thirty seconds to get the fuck out of my eyesight 'fore I change my mind."

By this time, a nice crowd had developed around the scene, and it was obvious that Peanut's manhood and pride were crushed from that episode by how he slowly strolled off. Marcus knew it would've been a costly move to blow Peanut's brains out in front of everyone on the block, but at the same time, deep down inside he knew it was a big mistake to show his pistol and not put it to use!

Chapter 19

Despite receiving several letters and recruitment calls from different Catholic schools, Chris rebelled and insisted on attending a popular public high school by the name of Westinghouse, which produced many college players over the years. Of course the athletic staff was extremely excited to be receiving one of the highest prospects out of the city since Mark Aguirre. Even a few of Chris's teammates and close friends followed suit and convinced their parents to allow them to attend the much more aggressive public school system.

"I'm tellin' you now; you do not wanna get on coach's bad side. Believe me, he'll put them hands on you in'a minute," One of the varsity players lectured Chris and his friends on their first day of school as they strolled down the crowded halls during the passing periods.

"Haaeeey, Chris!" a few gorgeous higher-classed young women seductively chanted as they passed by.

"Wassup!" Chris responded, immediately turning his attention in the direction that they were headed.

"You might as well forget about it," Chris's train of thoughts was interrupted by his fellow teammate. "Those hoes ain't nuttin' but'a distraction. They'll be the reason you won't make it far on this team. Believe me, I don seen it happened to the bests of'em."

What he thought was helpful advice; Chris took it as a form of jealousy. As they went their separate ways to attend their next class period, Chris spotted the young ladies entering the cafeteria. He and his friends glanced at each other before blurting out; "Fuck that!" as their attention quickly turned to having an early lunch period.

It was obvious that Chris was recruited to come in, being a positive impact to the basketball team, unlike most freshmen. In most cases, juniors and seniors are against freshmen, or what they call "fresh meat." They felt like freshmen should earn their spot on the team no matter who they were, instead of coming in, taking one of their positions. This situation was no different, and little did Chris know, he was in for a rude awakening!

"Man, I ain't tryn'a here that shit, cuz! Next time I see that nigga I'mma kill'em. That's on every thang I luv!" Peanut dramatically lashed out while speaking to his cousin, Spoonie, on the corner of Twenty-first and Homan.

"Listen, man! I gotta plan for that ma'fucka, jus' chill," Spoonie countered, attempting to calm his cousin's nerves. "Once I get him out the way, we'll have control over all this shit!"

"This muthafucka jus' put'a pistol in my mouth in front of everybody on Lawndale and you talkin' 'bout chill?" Peanut aggressively spoke with an expression of disbelief covering his face. "Look man, you gon' let me hold the thumpa' (gun) or what. I'm fenna' go get this nigga!"

As the two of them continued to discuss the situation, Spoonie was seriously contemplating on whether or not he should put himself in what he knew would be a bad predicament, even though Spoonie was jealous of the higher position Marcus was placed in, due to the fact that he was the one who gave Marcus his first hustling opportunity.

Spoonie knew in the back of his mind that it would be a huge loss to the nation if Marcus was prematurely killed; but at the same time, the other elites weren't as powerful as Marcus, nor did they have the mind-set of a chief, so he felt it was impossible for him not to be next to sit in the highest seat for the IVL nation.

146

In the midst of them going back and forth with each other, at the same time the both of them noticed the suburban truck that Marcus was last seen in, two blocks away, slowly driving down St. Louis. Marcus slowed down into a sudden stop when he saw Peaches walking down the street with her three kids.

"Wassup, baby!" Marcus shouted seductively while leaning toward the passenger side with his hands still steering the truck. In the same breath, he greeted all three kids, "Haeeey, Tierra, Shae-Shae, and Bri'!"

"Haeeey, Marcus!" all three children chanted back all at once.

"Marcus, can I have five dolla's?" Tierra, the oldest out of the three, blurted out innocently.

After everyone in the truck had a brief laugh from the innocent request, Marcus responded, "You sho'll can, baby. Come get it."

Tierra looked up at her mother, and after being given a nod of okay, she anxiously raced toward the truck; the other two followed suit. Marcus pulled out a thick knot of cash from his pocket and began peeling off ten-dollar bills for each kid. That's when Peaches hollered out, "Where mine at?"

"Baby, you know you can get whatever you want," Marcus replied sarcastically.

"Yeaah right!"

Since Marcus moved up in rank, his availability had been slim to none for Peaches. His class of women had escalated tremendously since he started making major money, but the fact still remained; for Peaches to be a female from the 'hood and stuck under 'hood circumstances, her beauty was on the same level as some of the women Marcus was involved with. Anytime Marcus would bump into Peaches while rotating in the streets, if she needed something, he gave it to her with no questions or strings attached because of the love he accumulated for her over the years. Peaches didn't mind not being Marcus's main lady; she understood how the game went. Her loyalty to Marcus still remained the same; whatever Marcus would ask of her, she would stop everything in a drop of a dime to get it done.

As the children happily marched their way from off the curb back onto the sidewalk where their mother stood, Peaches stated, "I what'nt playin'. Where mine at?" She said with a roll of the neck in a sassy manner.

"I'll be back through here later on to take care you."

"If I had a dollar for every time you told me that, I swear I'll be rich!"

"I'm for real. I'ma be in the neighborhood for'a minute. I gotta handle a few things."

"Whatever'! Come-on, y'all, let's go," She said with a slight attitude as she aggressively gathered her kids, preparing to walk off while the three of them were attempting to wave bye to Marcus.

Throughout the entire ordeal, Spoonie and his cousin Peanut stood where they couldn't be seen on Homan and quietly witnessed the whole scene. Before Marcus was able to pull off good, Peanut began applying more pressure to his cousin.

"Wassup up, cuz! Let me gon' ride down on this nigga. This the perfect time!" Peanut claimed as he spoke in a devilish tone while trying to convince Spoonie to give him a pistol.

Peanut was definitely a vicious killer and had been on plenty of missions for his respected mob from out of K-Town. Spoonie knew if he supplied Peanut the weapon that he was going to make something happen "by any means necessary." Even though they were affiliated with different organizations, they always were down for each other before anything.

"Shit!" Spoonie hollered out in an irritated tone while looking from side to side. "Do it right! I don't need this shit comin' back on me at all, you hear me?!" Spoonie angrily commanded while untucking the twelve-shot Glock nine from under his shirt.

"I got this shit," Peanut reassured him while attentively looking around while stuffing the pistol on his waistline. "When have you ever known me not to take care that bin'nis," he said while quickly backing his way toward his car.

Spoonie stood there emotionlessly as he watched Peanut burn rubber out of the parking space. Not only did he put his first cousin in harm's way, knowing how dangerous and risky the mission was, but he also jeopardized the growth of the nation by allowing an attempt on Marcus's life. Spoonie greed to have complete control over the nation was so great that it didn't matter whose life was on the line to make it happen, not even his own blood.

"Hello," Marcus answered a call with Lil G and Pee Wee riding alongside of him while driving down Sixteenth Street, a main street in the Holy City area.

"Yea, whudd up, boa'. Where ya at?" said the voice on the other end, obviously being that of Shawn's.

"Jus' bendin' a few blocks around Sixteenth. Wassup, everything a'ight?"

"Hell nawl. I need to get wit'chú as soon as possible."

"Meet me somewhere around here," Marcus said.

Before hanging up from each other, Marcus couldn't resist asking, "At least give me an idea on what this shit about?"

"Maaan, that nigga Dre had me meet him by the spot, right. When he pulled up, he gets out the car wit' B-lo"

The minute Marcus heard the name B-lo; he simply shook his head, sensing trouble.

"B-lo talking real reckless, telling me how I need to pay homage and some shit about keeping you and the rest of the lords from off Division."

"I knew them muthafuckas was gon' try to pull a stunt once we started making progress!" Marcus said harshly, turning the attention of everyone in the car to his phone conversation.

"I don't know, man . . . ," Shawn said with a sense of uneasiness. "But you know how that dude gets down. He don't give'a fuck about shit."

"So that right there should let'chú know what time it is," Marcus said, making references that a war was necessary.

"I was thinking we can sit down and talk someth—"

"Talk!" Marcus slightly snapped as he cut him off. "You know damn well that dude ain't tryn'a talk about shit! Aey, jus' hit my phone when you get in the area!"

Marcus seemed agitated after ending the call. From the conversation, Shawn seemed nervous and a bit timid. Marcus's reaction to the situation let it be known that he was down for whatever. His attention turned back to his guys in the car; they easily sensed a problem.

"Lord, what's wrong?" Pee Wee asked half breathing after taking a pull off the rotating blunt.

While reaching for the blunt, Marcus replied, "If it ain't one thing it's another, " He went on to explain. "It seem like since I took the seat, bullshit has been coming from everywhere. But'chú know it ain't nuttin' that can't get handled," Marcus said while giving off a slight stare in Pee Wee's direction before taking a pull off the blunt.

The three of them continued to rotate down Sixteenth as Marcus explained the situation about Shawn and the operation they had in progress across town on Division. Little did they know a crazed, pride-crushed Peanut had been trailing two cars behind the Suburban for the past four blocks.

"Bitch-ass nigga don met his match now," Peanut muttered to himself while puffing on a Newport with a .9mm pistol resting in his lap. "I'm fenna' wet his ass up!" he exclaimed in a devilish tone with the look of a lunatic in his eyes.

For the next three blocks, he patiently followed his target. Marcus made a sudden left turn onto Ridgeway, a side block off of Sixteenth Street.

Their conversation in the Suburban had lightened up from the previous talk of what needed to be done about the situation on Division. "Yeah, that hoe was tryn'a play hard to get at first. Now I got her ass hangin' by a string," Lil G stated in a pimpish manner from the backseat after ending a call from a young lady he encountered.

Before making it to the stop sign on Fifteenth and Ridgeway, one block down from Sixteenth, Marcus's phone rang in the midst of them talking.

"Yeah, where ya at, man?" Marcus answered in an irritated tone, recognizing the number before speaking through the receiver.

"I'm gettin' off at Independence right now," Said Shawn.

"Meet me in front of my momma house." As soon as Marcus instructed Shawn on where to meet him, he instantly made a sharp left turn on Fifteenth Street, not knowing possible trouble was directly behind him.

Peanut allowed a car to get behind the Suburban before making a left turn. Once turning onto Fifteenth Street, Peanut noticed his target turning left one block away onto Hamlin Street, the side block that would lead him to Marcus's mother's house on Nineteenth and Hamlin.

As he continued to pursue his mission, Peanut witnessed the Suburban get stalled up behind a car at a stale yellow stoplight that turned red seconds later.

"Showtime!" He hollered out with a crazed smirk covering his face as he cocked the nine.

Two cars ahead, Marcus and his guys had their mind set on the matter at hand. The situation that happened with Peanut on Lawndale earlier that day was momentarily erased out of their memory bank.

"Yeah, I might have to cut this sof'-ass nigga off," Marcus recited while ashing out the last of the blunt into the ashtray. Marcus and his two guys were so much into a zone from smoking some of the finest weed Chicago had to offer at the time; they didn't pay attention to the sounds of a car loudly burning rubber from afar. "This nigga sound like he scared to stand up for a spot that's making us damn near a hunit thousand a week!" he stated with a sense of disbelief.

Instead of Pee Wee having his eyes in the side mirror and out the window to be aware of their surroundings, he turned his attention in Marcus's direction to respond to the comment that was made. By the time the first few words was able to come out of Pee Wee's mouth, his entire thought process was interrupted by a '93 black four-door Cutlass Supreme. The car was able to slide up so closely to the Suburban that the driver could've actually reached out and touched the truck without getting out the car.

"Aey, lord!" Peanut yelled out while hanging the top half of his body outside the driver-side window with a mischievous grin covering his face.

In the motion of turning around to look out the passenger-side window, it was too late, the first rounds were

151

busting through the front and backseat windows viciously! Without having time to draw down his heat, all Pee Wee was able to do was try to get out of the line of fire.

"Awe shhhiiit!!!! I'm hit! I'm hit!" Were the words out of Pee Wee's mouth as he vigorously attempted to jump toward the backseat. Lil G was able to dodge the rapid shots by instantly falling facedown on the floor of the truck, but Pee Wee on the other hand wasn't so lucky. As he was wildly climbing his way to the back of the truck, bullets kept ripping the flesh of his back. In the midst of the shooting, Marcus somehow was able to swerve onto the sidewalk and burn rubber while making a left down Sixteenth Street, escaping the tirade of bullets. Before getting away from the scene, at least twelve rounds were fired inside the Suburban, leaving two shattered windows and a few holes on the interior.

"Lord, hurry up and get to a hospital. Wee back here fucked up, man!" Lil G spoke hysterically while Marcus drove a hundred miles per hour, swerving through traffic, running red lights, and even driving on the wrong side of the street, trying to make it to the nearest hospital in efficient time.

"Wee...hold on, man! Fight! Fight! I'm gon' get us there!" Marcus dramatically exclaimed while swerving through traffic like a madman on a police chase. "Lil G, hold his head up or some'nt! Keep'em breathing!" Marcus nervously demanded while taking slow, deep breaths himself.

"Hold on, Wee, man! We almost there, baby, hold on!!" Lil G spat out while holding Pee Wee's head in his lap.

By the expression on Pee Wee's face, he showed signs of being in a state of shock, and at the same time he was trying strongly to stay alive.

In the midst of pulling up to Mount Sinai's emergency room, Marcus began feeling a burning sensation coming from his abdominal area. When he glanced down, blood was gushing out of his side like a small river flow. He immediately put his hand down by his stomach, trying to make an attempt to stop the blood leak. Marcus's intensity level was so high from the bad condition Pee Wee was in that he ignored his pain and didn't realize he was hit.

After recklessly pulling up as close to the emergency room door as he possibly could, Marcus quickly jumped out the truck and limped his way inside the automatic sliding doors while grabbing hold to his right side.

"My friend out there dying! Somebody go out there and help'em please!" Marcus dramatically hollered out before staggering to the floor and passing out. Before the paramedics were able to make an effort to rescue Pee Wee, Lil G had him straddled in his arms, rushing him inside while demanding for help.

Chapter
20

"Baby, grab that phone for me," Steve yelled out to Sylvia on a pleasant evening while fixing around the house. "If it's Cee, jus' tell him to come-on through, I'm waiting on'em."

"Okaaay!" She responded while forcing herself out of her daily talk show program, *Oprah*.

Sylvia marched and turned toward the kitchen, mumbling a few disturbing words under her breath for being disrupted from her talk show.

"Hello," She answered in a formal tone.

"Uh . . . uh, haeey, Mrs. Williams," The person on the other end greeted nervously.

"Haeeey, whom am I speaking with?"

"This JR, ma'am. How you doing today?" JR replied with manners.

"JR . . . ?" Sylvia questioned as if she was caught off guard. "Boy, you ain't called my house since you and Marcus were kids," she chuckled out in between making her statement. "What, Marcus must've told you he was gonna be over here today or something?"

"No, ma'am. I was really calling to talk to Steve. Is he around?"

Before answering his question, she thought about it for a second. None of Marcus's friends ever called their house looking for Steve, so instinctively a sense of uneasiness began to overwhelm her. The intuition of a concerned mother started to kick in.

"Nawl! Baby, Steve ain't here," She said with an emotional distress forming upon her silky smooth caramel-complexioned face.

"What's the matter?"

"Well . . . uhhh—," JR stuttered out.

"JR . . . !" Sylvia began to snap after cutting him off, sensing trouble. "Stop beating around the bush and tell me know what the hell is going on!"

After hearing the loud commotion coming from the phone conversation, Steve headed in that direction to see what was the problem.

"Mrs. Williams, Mount Sinai Hospital jus' called my phone and told me that Marcus and Pee Wee was admitted into the emergency room after suffering from gun sh—"

"Oh God, oh God, oh my God! No, please Lord, nooooo!" Sylvia rapidly muttered out in a dramatic fashion after dropping the phone. Her nerves became so uncontrollably shaken from the news that she was unable to keep still as if she was having a nervous breakdown. Sylvia had both of her shaking hands wrapped around her mouth while tears were pouring down her face.

"Baby . . . !" He said while frantically attempting to console his wife. "What's wrong?"

From her hysterics, Sylvia wasn't able to clearly inform Steve on the news, so she pointed down at the phone, scared.

"Hello! Hello!" He furiously spoke through the receiver after picking the phone up from the floor, only to get the voice of the operator. "Sylvia! Who the hell jus' called this house!"

"It's Marcus, babe," She managed to cry out. "JR said he got'a call from the hospital saying Marcus been shot!" She said before letting out a hysterical cry.

"Shot . . . !" He shouted while showing signs of being in a semi–state of shock. "What hospital he at?"

"Mount Sinai."

"Come-on, let's go!" He said in the same motion of reaching for the car keys that rested on the kitchen table.

They both grabbed their jackets and raced for the door dressed as is.

On their ten-minute drive straight down Ogden Avenue to the hospital, Steve tried everything in his soul to console his wife. Sylvia was definitely in her concerned-mother mode as she rocked herself back and forth while constantly praying, trying to do everything to calm her nerves.

While pulling up to the hospital, they witnessed an unprecedented amount of people standing all around the hospital. The word had gotten around the west side almost faster than when the incident happened. Majority of the crowd were lords that were in deep rage from the incident and other people who just simply had much love for the two. There were even a lot of females from the neighborhood out there, crying and praying amongst each other. From the looks of the crowd, it seemed as if they all were gathered around to mourn the slaying of a world leader.

"What the hell going on up here," Steve blurted out, but not getting a response out of Sylvia who seemed numbed from the entire situation.

After double-parking on the side street due to the lack of legal parks because of the crowd, Sylvia and Steve rushed out their vehicle and began rambling through the crowd. Once a few people out of the crowd noticed who they were trying to get through, all that was heard was a loud commotion of voices demanding, "Everybody make a hole! Let chief momma and ole man get through!"

Within the rest of the rumbling voices, a group chanted out, "Unc, we gon' get them niggaz, believe that!" Steve managed to ignore the comments as they made it through to the main entrance.

"I'm sorry, we're not taking any more visitors," the receptionist said while stopping them in their tracks; the lobby was packed to capacity with concerned faces all around.

"Excuse me . . . ?" Sylvia began to snap. "We are the parents of a Marcus Williams and I was informed that he was being cared for here at this hospital!"

"Ma'am, I'm not sure if you are aware or not, but everyone here is trying to get the status of these two individuals. But I was informed not to give out any information."

After several demands from the crowd in the lobby and Sylvia and Steve going back and forth with the receptionist, she was forced to get someone of a higher position to come and allow them to be escorted to the floor of the intensive care unit area.

The nurse escorted them to the waiting room before going to get the operating surgeons. Once the two doctors made it to the room, one being of Oriental descent and the other white, they instantly began stating facts.

"Okay, to my understanding, you are the parents of," One of the doctors began to state before briefly checking his charts. "Marcus Williams."

"Correct," Sylvia replied nervously.

"Okay, ma'am, I'm going to cut right to the chase," The white surgeon began to explain. "Earlier this afternoon your son was able to maneuver his way to our emergency room despite being under extreme circumstances . . . Now I do have a little good news out of this terrible situation. Marcus is in stable condition, but his friend on the other hand wasn't so lucky. Do you have any information on Mr. Johnson's (Pee Wee) family?"

Sylvia hesitated before saying, "No . . . I mean, he has a grandmother but I wouldn't want to worry her like that, she's been through a lot and she's up in age. I look at Travis (Pee Wee) as a son figure, so you can feel free to talk to me about his condition."

"Well . . . ," The doctor began to comment in the midst of taking off his eyeglasses, "Me and the rest of my staff have been working continuously on keeping this young man alive. We actually had to revive him twice in order to keep him with us. He suffered from nine bullet wounds in the chest and back area while Marcus, in turn, took four, three in the abdominal area and one to the upper thigh area. While Marcus would still need to rehabilitate for a short period of time, Travis on the other hand would be lucky to walk again if he's able to make it through."

After receiving the news, Sylvia and Steve was relieved that Marcus was alive, but at the same time they felt just as bad for Pee

Wee. They had love for all of Marcus's closest friends as if they were their own.

"Doc, will we be able to see the both of them?" Steve asked.

"Yes. Marcus is responsive. But the tubes that we have running through him at this time won't allow him to talk very clearly. Now, Mr. Johnson is not responsive at all and he's breathing off of life support."

"Doc, please allow me to see Travis despite his condition. I would like to say a few prayers for his behalf. If you may?" Sylvia pleaded.

Before giving an answer, the two surgeons looked at each other before one spoke out, "Yes, I think we can make that happen, ma'am."

On their long walk down the cold hallways, all that was rambling through Sylvia's mind was how badly her son had been hurt. As they inched closer to the room door, the more nervous Sylvia became. Once entering the room, all of her emotions began to flare up again.

"Ohhhhh my baby!" Sylvia cried out with her hand covering her mouth as she rushed over to the bed area to embrace her firstborn as a mother would do a child. "Are you okay, baby?"

By Marcus being so weak from undergoing surgery, he managed to mumble out a few words while tightly gripping his mother's hand.

Instead of Steve being emotional about the situation, he stood in the background, mean mugging, as if he was gathering himself for a showdown.

"Marcus, baby, I need you to listen to me and listen to me good," Sylvia said while tearing up as she caressed her son's hand before lecturing him. "Baby, you need to really consider changing the way you live. I know you grown now, but you still my baby and I can't stand to lose you over some bullshit!" Sylvia cried out forcefully. "Marcus, I don't know if I'll be able to take another one of these episodes. It'll kill me!" she exclaimed in an even more dramatic fashion.

After making that comment, Marcus reacted by respectfully jerking his hand away from his mother's embrace and turning his face to hide the uncontrollable emotion. All the while, Steve stood back in silence.

"Well, baby, let me go check on your friend" She mentioned, immediately getting Marcus to face her again. "The doctor says he going to' make it, baby. The Good Lord blessed y'all." Before leaving out the room, she kissed Marcus on the forehead and said, "I'mma leave you and Steve alone while I go pray over Pee Wee."

The moment Sylvia stepped foot out the door, Steve marched over to the bed. Without asking Marcus how he felt, the first words out of Steve's mouth was, "I'mma make sure this shit get took care of befo' you check up out of this hospital! You hear me!" Steve dangerously assured.

Marcus repeatedly shook his head no at Steve's statement before clearly stating, "Pops, I need you to send word through to the streets, telling everybody to stay still and do not start a war ova' this shit." Marcus muttered this out while showing signs of weakness from the operation.

"Marcus," Steve hesitated. "You know how hard that's gon' be? Look out that window. Every nigga you see out there is ready to kill up the world for you!"

"Look!" Marcus strained out as he began to cough. After gathering himself, he continued, "Whoever did this shit tried to kill me and one of my brotha's in'a neighborhood we been in all our life! I'm gon' get to the bottom of this shit and make these niggaz feel my pain, personally!" Marcus stressed with great emotion as one cold tear slowly came rolling down his cheek.

Steve stood there speechless while staring at Marcus. Matching Steve's silence, Marcus turned his attention toward the window, which showed views of the roaring crowd outside of the hospital and also the Sears Tower and John Hancock Skyscraper that stood about fifteen miles away, deep into the downtown area.

A couple of minutes of being in a deep thought while staring down at the majority of his mob raising hell outside the hospital, most of them not knowing whether Marcus and Pee Wee were dead or alive, Marcus began to slowly nod his head up-and-down with a slight mysterious smirk forced upon his face. In the same motion, he glanced up at the towers, which landmarked the city, with a certain glare in his eyes as if to say, "This city belongs to me!" NOW!

Epilogue

Two weeks later . . .

After several operations and a few stitched-up wounds, Marcus was released out as an outpatient into the hands of Steve, Big C, Lil G, and a few other lords that were obviously there for extra protection. Marcus had to be escorted from the hospital to the car. The operations had him so weak to the point that he needed a urinal bag connected to his penis just for him to urinate properly. Pee Wee was picked up by his aunt and his baby mother. Although Pee Wee suffered a punctured lung and had to have it removed, he still managed to survive with all of his body parts being functional. After hearing the story on Pee Wee, people on the streets started looking at him damn near as a 2Pac figure; after dying twice and being brought back to life showed the real meaning of "real niggaz don't die"! Believe it or not, this situation boosted Pee Wee's popularity on the streets; and in the mind of thug niggaz, making it through this episode showed a great sign of strength.

With Steve on one side and Big C on the other, they helped escort Marcus out the hospital into one of Big C's low-key cars. Lil G was there to open the back door while Big C and Steve carefully placed him in the seat. Marcus looked quite rough from lying in the hospital for so long; he had grew out a thick and full beard and was in major need of a haircut.

After pulling off from the hospital with another car trailing behind them for security purposes, everyone in the car was in complete silence for a couple of minutes. With the radio turned off, all that was heard was the sounds of raindrops rapidly hitting the car from a grey and cloudy afternoon. Steve drove with Big C on the passenger side and Lil G in the backseat with Marcus. The minute or two of silence was broken when Steve asked, "How you feeling?"

"Better, now that I'm outta that damn hospital!" The statement made by Marcus helped lighten up the mood.

"I know how you feel, boa'. I get sick from jus' walking in that muthafucka," Big C responded in a semi humorous manner.

As they continued to rotate and make small talk, it looked as if they were heading in the direction of Marcus mother's house, which was minutes away from the hospital. Marcus noticed Lil G was silent during their conversation.

"Wassup, lord!" Marcus said, attempting to get some positive energy from his homey. Instead he got a simple nod of the head as a greeting. "You over there looking like you ready to go on'a rampage or some'nt. Everything gon' be a'ight," Marcus assured.

After giving Marcus a cold stare, Lil G broke his silence by stating, "I'm jus' glad to see my people make it through that shit." On their ride down Ogden Avenue, Marcus forced a few more words out of Lil G when he noticed Steve making a detour from the route to the house.

"Where we on our way to, ole man? We ain't going by the house?" Marcus asked curiously.

"I thought that maybe we'll take you somewhere that'll make you feel a little better," Steve answered.

"Pops, I ain't well enough to be getting no pussy, now. I'm still recovering," Marcus said in the midst of a mild laughter.

In between laughs, Steve replied, "I don't know, after seeing these two bitches, your condition might change.

After a couple more minutes of driving, they pulled up to their destination, which was only a couple of blocks away from where his mother lived. Before exiting the car, Marcus blurted out, "Pops, I know you ain't serious, man. I ain't in the mood to be fuckin' wit' no bitches!" Marcus dreadfully said. Without giving him a response, they all got out the car. Lil G and Steve helped Marcus to his feet while. While everyone else stayed put in the car that trailed behind them, the four of them walked toward a two-flat apartment building that Marcus wasn't familiar with. Marcus continued to talk against whatever he thought they had planned as he reluctantly made his way inside the first-floor apartment. Marcus started noticing that nobody was smiling as much, and Lil G seemed extremely focused on the situation.

As they entered the apartment, the three of them instantly guided Marcus downstairs to the basement that connected with the first-floor apartment. At that point, Marcus didn't know what to expect; all he knew was that his life was in good hands. Whatever they had planned, Marcus never feared for his life because in his mind, these were the same people that he was willing to put his life on the line for at any moment.

As soon as they stepped foot in the dark basement, Steve and Lil G began to turn on the lights. The sewage-scented basement was filled with large spider webs, rusted pipes, water leaks, old furnace and water heaters—a real grimy scenery.

Without saying a word, Lil G and Steve walked off from Big C and Marcus. They went into a room that was sectioned off and came back pushing two chairs that were occupied by two tied-up individuals with pillowcases covering their faces. From that moment on, Marcus knew that there was some real gangster shit in progress.

"Yeah son," Steve retorted. And for the first time, Marcus actually heard Steve call him son. "Do these niggaz look bitch enough for you?" He said with a smile as he and Lil G snatched the pillowcases off of the victims at the same time. Once uncovering their faces, Marcus recognized the two people to be Peanut and Spoonie; both of them were duct taped from their eyes down to their mouth.

Marcus stood there emotionlessly with an expression that definitely showed signs of revenge. Marcus slowly limped his way toward the two. When he got close enough, Steve presented him with a six-shot chrome .38 revolver with the rubber grip before saying, "This what'chú asked for, right. Now do the honors." After making that statement, Marcus forcefully snatched the duct tape from each one of their eyes, one at a time. Without either one of them being able to say anything, their eyes told the whole story. Once Spoonie saw Marcus's face, he instantly busted out into a major sweat, with his eyes opened wide, trying to wiggle himself out of the tightly wrapped rope, attempting to explain himself. Peanut, on the other hand, looked very calm and collected, letting it be known that he was ready to die. Marcus stood there with the pistol in hand and stared at Spoonie as he was struggling, before snatching the tape off his mouth.

"Marcus! Listen to me, lord, please!" Spoonie began to plead his case in a very dramatic way. "I tried everything in my power to stop'em, lord. He didn't wanna listen! I would never do nuttin' to jeopardize the nation, you know that shit!" he hollered out with his voice being overwhelmed by a manly outcry. *Smack!!!* Lil G swung with all his might, hitting Spoonie across the mouth with his pistol.

"Shut the fuck up!" Lil G aggressively demanded, showing signs of a true enforcer.

With blood gushing from his mouth, Spoonie managed to scream out, "I made y'all, niggaz!" He continued to hysterically cry out, "If it what'nt for me, y'all niggaz wouldn't be shit! You hear me! Y'all wouldn't be shit!" Spoonie saw Marcus's hand slowly raising the pistol to his face, and that's when the panic attack kicked back in. "Come-on, Marcus, man, don't do this shit! Cee, talk to'em! This shit is against the laws! I'mma muthafuckin' five-star universal, y'all can't jus' do this shit to me!" Before Spoonie was able to say another word, Marcus let off two shots that left perfect holes in Spoonie forehead, leaving him laid on his back, tied up, with his eyes wide open, staring at the ceiling. Seconds later Lil G followed suit, but instead of two neat holes to the face, Lil G went on a rampage by emptying his thirteen-shot clip in the face of Peanut, leaving a mess!

After the last shots were fired, Marcus looked back at Big C and Steve with no remorse in his young eyes. Big C simply gave off a nod of approval as Marcus dropped the gun and limped his way toward the way they entered. Lil G stayed behind as the two of them helped Marcus back to the car while swiftly trying to escape the extreme raindrops that was falling. When they successfully made it inside the car, the other carload of people began heading toward the building. Now it was clear to see that they were the cleanup crew!

The Saga Continues with . . . . The Holy City, Part II "Rise in Power"

Made in the USA
Charleston, SC
19 May 2013